D1038186

Donated to
INCORPORATED
1893

OUT OF REACH

CARRIE ARCOS

Simon Pulse
New York London Toronto Sydney New Delhi

This book is a work of fiction. Any references to historical events, real people, or real locales are used fictitiously. Other names, characters, places, and incidents are the product of the author's imagination, and any resemblance to actual events or locales or persons, living or dead, is entirely coincidental.

SIMON PULSE

An imprint of Simon & Schuster Children's Publishing Division

1230 Avenue of the Americas, New York, NY 10020

First Simon Pulse hardcover edition October 2012

For information about special discounts for bulk purchases, please contact Simon & Schuster Special Sales at 1-866-506-1949 or business@simonandschuster.com.

The Simon & Schuster Speakers Bureau can bring authors to your live event. For more information or to book an event, contact the Simon & Schuster Speakers Bureau at 1-866-248-3049 or visit our website at www.simonspeakers.com.

Designed by Mike Rosamilia

The text of this book was set in Adobe Caslon Pro.

Manufactured in the United States of America

2 4 6 8 10 9 7 5 3

Library of Congress Cataloging-in-Publication Data

Arcos, Carrie.

Out of reach / Carrie Arcos.

p. cm.

Summary: Accompanied by her brother's friend Tyler, sixteen-year-old Rachel ventures through San Diego and nearby areas seeking her brother, eighteen-year-old Micah, a methamphetamine addict who ran away from home.

ISBN 978-1-4424-4053-1

[1. Brothers and sisters—Fiction. 2. Methamphetamine—Fiction. 3. Drug abuse—Fiction. 4. Runaways—Fiction. 5. California, Southern—Fiction.] I. Title.

PZ7.A67755Out 2012

[Fic]—dc23

2011044501

ISBN 978-1-4424-4055-5 (eBook)

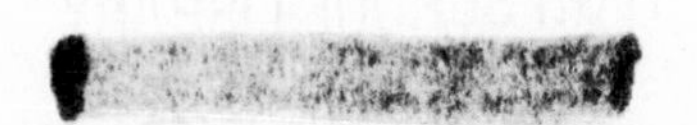

For Nathan

Chapter One

The first time my mom told me liars didn't go to heaven was when she tried to get me to confess to hitting my eight-year-old brother. I was seven. She had knelt down in front of the brown leather couch where the two of us sat at opposite ends. Micah hugged his left arm—evidence of the deed still a bright red mark an inch or so above his elbow. He whimpered for effect, while I remained stubbornly silent. After waiting for some time, my mom stood up and said very softly, "You know, liars don't go to heaven."

My mom used this phrase throughout my childhood, expecting it would be a deterrent to bad behavior. She didn't know that the thought of pearly white gates, white mansions, and an eternal soundtrack of harps disturbed me. I mean, who even listens to harp music? And then there was the singing. I'm sure angels' voices are beautiful and everything, but how long would I be expected to sing? What about the people who were tone deaf? Did that change when they passed on?

What kind of food would we eat? What if we didn't *get* to eat? I was terrified of being sent to a place where I thought I'd be bored out of my mind after ten minutes.

Besides, lying came naturally. "Who ate the last cookie?" I'd point to my brother. "Where did my money go?" Cut to me shrugging. "Are her parents going to be there?" My head nodded on cue, though I knew her parents were away for the weekend.

I learned to lie by watching Micah. He'd keep his amber-brown eyes steady and look Mom straight in her eyes. He didn't smile or talk too much to give himself away. He remained calm, quiet even. The trick, he told me, was that a part of him actually believed the lies.

He took me under his wing, and we began covering for each other. I didn't tell Mom or Dad where he was or what he was doing, and he didn't tell them whom I secretly dated or when I came home late. We had an unspoken pact. We lied to our parents with ease. We lied to our teachers. We even lied to each other.

The truth? Everyone lies. Every single person. Even my mom. When Micah didn't come home one night, she looked at me the following morning and told me he went to visit my uncle in the Bay Area for the summer. She said the change of scene would do him good, and then she raised her left hand to her temple. The subtle movement was her tell. I knew her signs, having studied her my whole life, as if we played some high-stakes poker game together, even if the winnings meant only that I got to stay up a half an hour later.

I thought Micah had bailed for the night and crashed at some friend's house like the last time. I didn't allow my thoughts to take me to the darker places. But when I walked into his room and saw his guitar stand lying on its side next to his unmade bed, I knew. His Cali Girl case was gone. He had taken his Gibson Les Paul. I stood in the middle of his room very aware of the silence surrounding me and understood that heaven must be a big empty space.

Sometimes I couldn't sleep. I'd hear these sounds through the wall between Micah's and my bedrooms. Light feet on the floor. Pacing. The squeaking of his old bed. More pacing. Another roll of springs grating on metal. The quiet strum of his guitar. The whispered conversations to God knows who. His door opening at hours when it should've been closed. I eventually started sleeping with a small fan on next to my bed to block out all the sounds. It helped, mostly.

My parents first asked me about Micah and drugs a little over a year ago. They wanted to know when it started. I lied. I told them I didn't know. I told them I knew he'd experimented here and there, but I didn't think it was anything serious. I pretended I was as shocked as they were.

I didn't tell them that the first time Micah used meth was at a party he'd played with his band over two years ago. While he'd tuned his guitar, someone had given him a small white pill and told him it would take the edge off. Classic. He took it and didn't sleep for two days. I knew because I heard him through the thin wall. A couple of days later, after finally sleeping it off, Micah strolled nonchalantly into my room and started touching the books on my shelf, which usually meant he was in a talkative mood.

"You gonna say anything?" Of course he knew that I knew. He didn't even try to insult me with a lie.

"What?" I said.

"It was only one time."

"I know."

He pulled out *The Stranger*, a depressing book I'd had to read the year before and had enjoyed simply because I could check it off my list for the "college bound."

"It's weird." Micah fanned through it, stalling, looking for words. "I felt . . . it was . . . the best I've ever felt. This super rush. I didn't know I could ever feel that way. Like I could do anything, you know?"

"No, I don't know." I didn't mean to stifle his moment, but I didn't want to encourage him either.

He looked at me like I was the little sister who didn't know anything, put the book back on the shelf, and left the room.

I walked over and returned the book to its proper place. If I had known that his mind had already been altered with that first try, that the seed of addiction had taken root, maybe I would have done more. Maybe. But I didn't.

Micah claimed he used as an artistic experience, saying that he connected with the universe when he was high. He used to create. He used to perform. He said it gave him his magic mojo, like he became some kind of different entity, some superpower. But that was in the beginning. Eventually he needed it to function. No one noticed, or maybe they didn't want to notice, the change. He was the usual warm body in class. His grades weren't great, but they never had been. But he soon turned from my older brother into a walking cliché.

Maybe if I'd sent an anonymous letter to my parents in the beginning, everything could have been avoided. We could have had an intervention, like the one I watched on TV where the family and two friends sat in a living room and ambushed the guy when he walked into the room.

The guy said, "Hell no!" over and over again, along with a few other expletives that I could read on his lips, though they were edited out for TV.

By the end of the half hour he was crying and hugging his mom. The mediator was all smiles. I could have been the hero of the family. Instead, I lied and told myself that it was just a phase. Micah would be able to quit when he wanted to. Now I carry that burden.

* * *

Mom and Dad had supported Micah doing the band thing, even showed up at some of the gigs. My dad bought him his first guitar. They'd more than tolerated his colored hair and the tattoo he got right before senior year. When the school called about his missing classes, they had a more serious talk around the kitchen table. By that time, they were witnessing the effects of his habitual drug use, but they had no idea how bad it really was. They forced him to attend one substance abuse meeting, and he returned saying he'd seen the light and wouldn't use anymore. But I overheard him telling someone on the phone that the people there were all old, and losers. That they were nothing like him.

After Mom found some crystals at the bottom of one of Micah's drawers, she and my dad formulated a new plan. They gave him an ultimatum. They told him he had to go to rehab—a six-week program designed for teens ages twelve to eighteen. They said they were employing tough love, something they had learned from a book and a TV talk show. Only seventeen at the time, a minor, Micah had to go.

As part of the program, my parents attended weekly group sessions. They thought it best that I not go, out of concern for Micah's comfort. I'm sure he felt so comfortable living and sharing his innermost, deepest feelings with strangers. Whatever. I stayed home or hung out at Michelle's.

Besides, I had my own problems to deal with. Namely, Keith.

We had almost broken up, and I didn't really want to get into it with my parents. My mom loved Keith. He had that way, that charm with women of all ages. It began with an infectious smile that spread to his eyes as he looked at you. Mom gladly fell victim to it every time. Keith's smile even worked on teachers, male and female, which was why he never had to worry about making grades to stay on the baseball and basketball teams.

But him getting with Marcie Armstrong? I could have gotten some disease. Keith told me it was a one-time thing, just some party that had gone out of control. Marcie had thrown herself on him, and he said he was too drunk to even remember what had really happened. He actually had tears in his eyes when he told me. That killed me. I held him and whispered that it'd be okay; we'd figure it out. I ignored the small thing that felt like it was dying inside.

When I'd ask my parents how it went after a session, they'd always give the same answer, "Your brother is going to be fine." Then the TV would turn on and my dad would sit in front of it and my mom would take the stairs to their room. I'd disappear and remain invisible until the morning rush to school and work.

I was surprised when they asked me to go to one of Micah's sessions. I didn't really want to, but they said it would be good for our whole family.

It played out something like this . . .

We entered a large white office with pictures of nature above motivational slogans like "Life is a journey, not a destination" and "Opportunity will arise when you ride the wall of change" hanging from the wall. Metal chairs formed a circle in the center of the room. People I did not know, except for Micah, looked up at us and nodded when we entered the room. We were late. The counselor or shrink, whatever he was, invited us to sit down. His dreads flopped about when he turned his head and indicated a chair. I sat below a picture of a sunset. Its caption read: "Today is the first day of the rest of your life. Make it happen!"

The session began with the counselor leading everyone in a kind of prayer. "God grant me the serenity to accept the things I cannot change, courage to change the things I can, and wisdom to know the difference."

It was weird. I didn't know they had sent Micah to a religious thing. My family didn't go to church, like Michelle's. Mom was raised Catholic, so we got dressed up and went to Mass on Easter Sunday, when we'd hear sermons that were mostly the same year to year, something about death and Jesus.

Mom enjoyed the music. Dad liked it when the priest was funny. Micah liked the part where they tortured and killed Jesus, which was the part that bothered me the most. I thought it strange that people believed in a God who could watch His son be killed, although I supposed He seemed tame in comparison to all the Greek gods. At least Jesus didn't have His insides pecked out by a vulture for eternity.

Church didn't make much sense to me. And then there was the whole problem of evil and suffering in the world, and child molesters, and zits. Michelle had tried explaining it once, but again, I didn't really see the point.

Religion would leak from my mom every now and then in a series of catchphrases she'd learned growing up, like liars not going to heaven or "for the love of all that's holy," or "sweet Mary, mother of Jesus." Sometimes I'd catch her making the sign of the cross, her hands performing the ritual out of muscle memory more than anything else.

When I was really young, I gave God a name. I called him Frank. I don't know why, the name just seemed to fit. Even Micah started calling him that. Mom became nervous because of its being sacrilegious or something, so we eventually stopped. I didn't speak to Frank for years. But a couple of nights after Micah left, I tried to talk to Frank. I asked him to find Micah, to help out. I tried to take back what I had secretly wished, the part about wanting Micah to disappear.

I waited in the dark of my bedroom, but Frank didn't say anything. I wasn't that surprised because Frank had always been more of a listener, a bit evasive, mysterious—kind of like socks that go missing from the washer to the dryer. One moment I thought He was there, the next I found myself groping around in the dark for the intangible missing sock. In my opinion, God didn't really have anything to do with what had been going on with Micah, but I figured it didn't hurt to ask for His help.

Peace. Serenity. I remembered that one from an SAT list.

How was there peace in accepting what couldn't be changed? I heard my parents and Micah stumbling through the words. Micah slouched a bit in his chair. His long legs stretched across the floor and crossed at the ankles.

After the opening prayer, those who were part of the rehab program were asked to share what they had been learning, what they had been feeling with their families.

A girl named Mandy spoke first. Her long black hair masked half of her face but revealed a black eye that fluttered around like a bird as she talked. She looked my age, sixteen, although she seemed older because she was skinny, real skinny. Anorexic skinny. Her face sunk in on itself, giving the illusion of a model's high cheekbones. Her mouth stretched to cover large white teeth that hung from her gums. Every so often she pulled her lips back and made a sucking sound as she swallowed the spit.

Mandy confessed to the group and her parents that she used to sleep with guys to get heroin. She didn't have a number, just that there were a lot of men, and an occasional woman. She'd already had some kind of STD, and she was trying to work up the courage to get tested for AIDS.

The girl sitting next to her, who could have been her twin with her same too-skinny look, held her. Mandy's mother smiled encouragingly, revealing her own large horse teeth.

"Thank you, Mandy. That was very brave of you today." The counselor responded with a heavy kindness. He shuffled his loafers underneath his chair, and I couldn't make his dreadlocks and the loafers work together in my mind.

All of the inmates, or residents—I wasn't sure what to call them—then took a turn sharing something with their family members in the circle. Each story sounded similar, with the details shaken like we were playing a big game of Boggle. After someone shared, questions were asked or encouraging comments given. The counselor always thanked the person speaking. There was something awkward in the release of so much emotional pain, but it had also been cathartic. It meant no more hiding. No more secrets. No more telling lies. My right foot bounced on the bottom rung of the chair. I didn't want to be there.

"Micah, you've been a little quiet today," the counselor said suddenly, turning to face my brother.

Micah shrugged and slouched a bit more in his chair.

"I see your whole family came today."

"Yep." He didn't look up at us.

"Is there anything you'd like to say?"

Micah looked like he wanted to hit the guy in the face, but he restrained himself. He hesitated and said, "I've gradually been siphoning off my college fund to, you know, pay for things."

"Pay for what, Micah?" the counselor asked.

Micah sucked in some air, clearly annoyed. "For the meth."

Dad went rigid in his chair. This was clearly new information to him. "How much did you take?"

Micah stared at the ground, and I followed his gaze. I imagined the white tile, cool against my face if I could just lie down and close my eyes. If I could just lie down and escape the pulsing in my head.

"All of it." The next words came in a rush, strung together. "I'm sorry. I'll pay it back. All I need are a couple of shows when I get out of here. The guys say some people are really interested."

"We've been saving that for years." The words hissed out of Dad's mouth.

"I said I'd pay it back," Micah whispered.

Mom placed her hand on Dad's leg.

"Fine," he said. "You'll pay it back."

"Maybe he can get a scholarship," she offered.

Dad grunted. "A little late for that."

"Maybe I won't go to college," Micah said in the same subdued voice. "I mean, my grades aren't that great. I'm not smart like Rachel."

When I heard my name, I picked my head up, annoyed that my attempt at invisibility had been foiled.

"You are just as smart as Rachel, honey," my mom said. "You've just gotten a little sidetracked." She spoke of his addiction as if it were a small speed bump on a suburban street. "When this is all put behind us, you'll see. Next year you'll be in college. It'll be so much better."

"You're not listening to me." Micah sat up in his chair. He

grasped his hands in front of him and spoke very slowly. "I'm not going to college. I don't want to go. After graduation, I'm going to LA with the guys."

Dad couldn't hide his anger anymore. "The guys? What are you going to do? Play music on the streets? How are you going to live? You've got a serious problem here that you're not even dealing with."

The counselor tried to interject, "Now, Mr. Stevens, I think it's important that we allow Micah to express his—"

Dad cut him off. "I'm tired of all of this psychobabble. Micah, this isn't you. It's the drugs talking. I get that. I really do. This isn't you. When you get out of here, we can talk about this some more."

"You're not listening to me!" Micah yelled.

Then everything became quiet.

"Go on, Micah, tell us what you're feeling." The counselor spoke softly, but looked at my dad with threatening eyes.

Micah started out slowly. "This is me. I'm not you or Mom. I know I have some issues, but I've got it handled now. I'm fine." And then he said the biggest lie ever. "I'm not perfect like Rachel."

The shock must have registered on my face because the counselor asked me, "Rachel, is there anything you'd like to say to Micah? It's okay. This is a safe space."

Safe spaces exist only where people aren't, I thought. I shook my head, no.

"You sure?" the counselor said, prodding. This time his dreads reminded me of small snakes, coiling and uncoiling. Micah looked in my direction. He hadn't changed. His brown eyes still held the same dead expression as they had since he'd chosen meth over everything else in his life.

My mouth made a smile. "It'll be good to have you home," I lied.

The funny thing about a lie is that once it has been said and believed, it lives and becomes. It can't be taken back. It sucks all the air from you until you give up and it takes over and you forget how to breathe on your own. It is like those parasitic relationships, but not like the shark and the little remora that politely cleans the shark's skin and sometimes attaches itself to its underbelly. No, it is more like a tapeworm eating someone from the inside out.

My AP bio teacher caught one when he lived somewhere in South America for a summer. He came home and started feeling sick and couldn't gain any weight. Turns out, he had a twenty-foot tapeworm feeding and growing in his intestine. He knew we wouldn't believe him, so he brought some of it to class in a jar, where it floated, looking like the longest piece of linguini I had ever seen.

How gross was that? He had actually asked the doctor if he could keep the tapeworm when they removed it.

Just like a tapeworm, sometimes a lie has to be physically removed. The problem is, most of us still carry the lie around inside a jar like a souvenir.

Chapter Two

Tyler was waiting for me when I pulled into the 7-Eleven parking lot. He leaned against his truck, smoking a cigarette. The clock on my dashboard read 8:55.

Early for a stoner, I thought. I took it as a good sign.

I pulled alongside him, kept the car running, and rolled down my window. "Hey."

"Hey." He took another hit, threw the cigarette down, and smashed it into the pavement with the ball of his right foot. The smoke left his parted lips like a slow-moving fog. He pushed his straight black hair, which hung slightly over the top of his eyes, away from his face and looked across the parking lot. "You sure you're ready for this?"

I followed his gaze to another car that had pulled in. I recognized the driver, who stepped out of the car wearing the store's employee uniform. He had graduated with Micah's class in June.

"Yes."

Tyler opened the driver's side of his truck and grabbed a black backpack. He shut the door, locked it, and walked slowly around the front of my car. He wore his usual ensemble: Hollister jeans, which hung a little low at the waist; a black T-shirt; and a chain of keys looped to one of the buckles. He was a year younger than Micah, like me, though he was taller than Micah, probably close to six feet. Tyler had that long, lean build, perfect for soccer and playing the bass, both of which I knew he did well. He was cocky, too, walking as if he expected me to watch him. The passenger door to my Civic opened, and he slid inside with that familiar ash smell.

"I just have one rule. No smoking in the car." I looked him in the eyes, hoping he would see that I was serious.

"All right. Here's my rule. No bitching about me smoking." His expression matched my own.

I looked away first, shifting the gear to reverse. "Glad we have an understanding." I pulled out of the parking lot.

"May I?" He motioned to the stereo.

"Sure, whatever." I kept my eyes on the road as Morrissey's voice filled the space between us. A fitting melancholy set in.

"Not bad," he said.

"You're not the only one who knows music." Tyler was in

Micah's band, which meant he probably thought he was some kind of expert, like Micah. I didn't feel like making small talk, but I didn't want to be a jerk. "Thanks for helping me find him."

Tyler moved the seat back and put on his dark sunglasses. "I'm not making any promises."

"I know."

From the little I knew of Tyler, he seemed to speak the truth, and that was something I needed. No more bullshit. No more lies. "I just mean you didn't have to."

"Yeah. Well"—he shifted in his seat—"he owes me money."

I hadn't known that, but I wasn't surprised. *Micah owes me, too,* I thought, *much more than just money.* I turned onto the ramp to the 15 Freeway heading south toward San Diego.

"Watch it!" Tyler yelled.

I swerved just in time to avoid a black Lexus coming up on the left.

"Need me to drive?" he asked, sitting up straight. Out of the corner of my eye, I could see him turn toward me.

"I'm fine, really. Why don't you take a nap?" With the traffic in front of us, it was going to be a while. "It's gonna take at least an hour to get there."

"Over an hour." Tyler laid his head back and folded his bronzed arms across his chest.

I could see the bottom half of the Aztec eagle sketched into his arm. The sleeve of his black T-shirt covered the rest, but I knew it was there. He'd gotten it done when he went through his *La Raza* phase. He'd spent last summer down in Mexico with relatives, came back speaking some Spanish and talking about oppression, and how corrupt American politics were. He staged a walkout of his history class right before Thanksgiving break, objecting to the term Indian and even Native American, saying they should be called by their tribal names. He even got the whole school chanting the name of the tribe who'd helped the pilgrims, whatever it was.

I kind of liked that side of Tyler, but it didn't last long. Keeping up with a cause was exhausting, I supposed, when you were in high school and the bass player in a band. Besides, once Christmas came around, it was all Santa and elves and carols. No one wanted to hear about how California should really be part of Mexico. No one cared.

I couldn't believe it was already August, with only a couple of weeks left before I started my senior year. The fact that Micah was still missing was a subject that everyone tiptoed around like a kid avoiding cracks on a sidewalk. No one asked me about him, but they gave sad smiles. The kind you gave at funerals when you pass the family in the receiving line. The kind given when you don't really know what to say.

It didn't matter. I had decided to move on. It had been a couple of months, and college applications cried for my attention. I didn't have time to wallow in the fact that Micah had left us; that he had left me without so much as a word. In my opinion, I had already given him enough of my time. And then I got the e-mail.

Rachel,

You do not know me, but I know who you are. We have a mutual acquaintance, your brother, Micah. He's not doing so good. He's living on the streets, playing guitar for money, among other things. He's in trouble, not the kind you can get out of so easily, if you know what I mean. But the more serious shit, the kind where someone could get themselves hurt or . . .

He'd be upset if he knew I wrote you. He talks about you the most. That's got to mean something, right?

Anyway, he's in Ocean Beach.

I read the e-mail a couple of times, printed it out, and stuffed it into the drawer in the table by my bed where I kept lists and other things. Another week went by before I read it again. This time, I approached it like a text in my English class. I looked for patterns. I dissected the words. What did "not doing so good" mean? *Good* was such a relative term. What kind of trouble was he in? I imagined the "or . . ." signified something beyond hurt, which meant the person who sent the e-mail thought my brother's life was in danger.

But who sent the e-mail? I was pretty sure it didn't come from someone at school, unless it was a cruel joke. It had to be someone who knew him, someone he trusted. I tried to trace it, but it was sent from some generic Hotmail account, as if anyone even used Hotmail anymore.

Two sentences kept coming back to me. *He talks about you the most. That's got to mean something.* I knew it had to be a lie. Micah had barely spoken to me, let alone acknowledged my presence, during the weeks before he left. But what lay behind the lie disturbed me. Someone was worried about my brother, and knew my weakness: guilt. It was the one weapon I had no defense against.

I tried sleeping that night but couldn't, so I called Tyler, the only friend of Micah's I could stand, the following day and read him the e-mail over the phone.

He was silent for a moment, and then asked me to read it again. When I finished, I said, "Well?"

"Cryptic."

"I'm going," I said.

"When?"

"Tomorrow."

I heard him suck in some air and let it out in one huge rush. "All right."

Our plan was simple: Leave early in the morning, drive down to Ocean Beach in San Diego, look for Micah, and be home by eight, as my parents expected. In my mind, only one scenario could play itself out: We find Micah sitting on the sidewalk with his guitar and a can, asking for money. When he sees us, he is argumentative at first, but quickly apologizes and thanks us for finding him. On the way home, he worries about what he'll say to Mom and Dad, but we both reassure him that we'll be there for him. I block out any other versions of what might go down.

The car started the long climb out of the valley where we lived. As it reached the top of the hill and started down the other side, I saw the wide four-lane freeway snake off into the distance. We had a long way to go.

By the sound of his breathing, I could tell Tyler was already asleep. I glanced at him. His knees crushed against the dashboard as he slouched in his seat. His lips formed a lopsided grin before he mumbled something I couldn't quite make out. A sleep talker. *Good,* I thought. *Maybe I'll get some dirt on him.*

My fingers drummed the steering wheel to the rhythm of the music. On either side of us were brown hills, covered with boulders of all shapes and sizes.

When Micah and I were younger, Mom used to have us pretend we were in an old Western as we drove past the rocky hills. She'd point in a direction and say, "Look out, I see one now." We'd duck in the car, as if we could see the top of a black cowboy hat, and would imagine the bad guy hiding behind the rock with his rifle. Micah and I would take our turns aiming and firing at him. One of us reloaded while the other fired, until Mom warned us about another imaginary cowboy and we'd switch our aim. We'd always make it through the pass. Sometimes Micah or I pretended that we'd gotten a small flesh wound, but there were never any casualties. As we drove away from the "hill country," as Mom called it, she would speak of the bad guy who'd gotten away and how he'd be waiting for us the next time.

This was how we passed our time during family road trips; sometimes we were pioneers out West, and other times we were explorers on another planet. My mom loved to play "let's pretend." The games lasted even into junior high, where we humored her because we still kind of wanted to be kids and have fun.

By the time Micah entered high school, however, he let us know that playing make-believe games with our mom was not cool. Since I measured most things against his opinion, I stopped playing too. Mom eventually succumbed to our silent treatments and eye rolls. Car trips became competing playlists, as Micah and I sat in the backseat with headphones on, staring out the side windows at nothing more than rocks on a brown hill.

Micah became cool sophomore year when Missy Eyers asked his band to play at her party. Since she was a senior and a cheerleader, Micah received instant status. To be fair, he had been rising pretty steadily on his own merit, but the Missy gig propelled him over the top. All I heard (because I didn't get to go, I was only a freshman at the time) was how awesome they were, how cute Micah was, and how he and Missy made out and probably did it. Micah confirmed the first, but was purposefully elusive on the third.

His band became the official party band. They also started playing shows in local clubs, some even twenty-one and over. They had to wear a wristband that said they couldn't drink. Everyone said they were going somewhere. What they really meant was that Micah was going somewhere. He was the band's magic. Seeing Micah in front of a mic with his guitar, you knew he was going to be somebody.

He became somebody, just not the somebody we all thought. Micah wasn't some teenage loser who had fallen into the drug pit. He had a desired commodity; he had potential. When we all started to see him throw that away, that was the hardest to take.

At school, I heard the whispered *Why?* in clusters of students, former friends, or admirers. Teachers shook their heads in disappointment. They pulled me aside to tell me that they were "here for me" if I needed anything, which I thought was strange because wasn't it their job to "be there" for me already?

Why was Micah screwing up and throwing his life away? Why did he bail on all of us? I had no answer. Why did it have anything to do with me?

I was lost in thought when the car in front of me stopped suddenly, and I had to slam on the brakes. I braced myself for the hit from behind, but it didn't come. Tyler stirred next to me. He rolled his body toward the window of the passenger seat and mumbled, "Tell me something I don't know." I could see the tops of blue plaid boxers over his jeans.

I focused on the road in front of me and decided that when we found Micah, I would ask him, "Why?" but no matter what answer he gave, I knew I'd still want to punch him in the face.

Chapter Three

"Now what?" I asked Tyler.

The streets of Ocean Beach all looked the same to me, small and cramped with tiny wooden cottages painted in different pastels. The gray clouds didn't help, as they gave everything a dark, ominous feeling. I didn't know where to go.

"Coffee," he said, and sat up. His voice sounded rough and deep, like he needed water, not coffee. He rubbed his face with his hands and then through his hair.

"Coffee?"

"Yeah, there's a shop on the corner of Newport. We'll start there."

I didn't think Micah would be sitting at a coffee shop, but I didn't have any better ideas.

Tyler directed me to one of the side streets where there were plenty of two-hour parking spots. As I turned off the car's engine, I glanced at the dashboard. We had until 12:38.

Tyler reached into his bag and shoved a hunter-green Mao hat on his head and turned to smile at me. In the morning light, the hat appeared to match the color of his eyes.

"Your eyes are green," I said. I hadn't noticed how green they were before, almost like a pale forest green.

"Last I checked." He smiled, revealing dimples in both cheeks, and bent quickly to stuff his bag under the seat. He opened the door and got out of the car.

I got a text from Michelle wondering if we had found Micah yet. I texted her back to tell her we'd only just arrived, then shut off my phone and put it in the glove compartment. I didn't want to deal with people texting and calling me. I brought my backpack, though. It was practically empty, except for sunscreen, a light black hoodie, my wallet, and a notepad.

"Okay, Frank," I said to the empty car. "Please help me find him." It couldn't hurt to ask.

The coffee shop was on the main street that led to the ocean. Opening the door, I scanned inside for Micah, but saw only a couple of people scattered near outlets working on laptops, an older man reading a paper, and two women talking at a small table. Even though I knew he probably wouldn't be kicking back and sipping a cappuccino, I couldn't help feeling disappointed. If I wanted to survive the day, I knew I'd have to have realistic expectations. Those expectations would probably exclude hope.

The perky barista took Tyler's order.

"You guys together?" she asked.

"No," Tyler said, and moved aside so I could order a latte.

A woman in a long flowered dress and no shoes shuffled in with her head down and made her way past us in the direction of the bathroom.

"Excuse me?" the barista said. "I'm sorry, but you can't use that. It's only for customers."

The woman didn't stop. She tried opening the door, but it was locked.

"You need a key to use it, and I'm sorry, but the manager won't let us open it for you."

The woman muttered a few words at the floor. She stood in front of the bathroom door and rocked from the balls of her feet to her heels and back again. Her long hair shielded most of her face.

"Can I have another small coffee?" Tyler asked.

"Sure," the girl said, and rang him up.

"It's for her." Tyler motioned to the woman, who still stood in front of the bathroom door with the FOR CUSTOMERS ONLY sign.

The barista gave Tyler an annoyed look, but reached in a drawer and handed Tyler a token, along with his coffee. He opened the door for the woman and gave her the coffee.

"Who knew Tyler had a sweet side?" I said to him as we left with our drinks. "Don't worry, I won't tell."

He ducked his head and took a sip of his coffee. "Mmm. Nothing like a cup of joe to put some hair on your chest."

"Not really what I'm aspiring for." I laughed as I fell into step beside him.

We walked south toward the beach on the main street, which was lined with tall, emaciated palm trees. The usual beach clothing, surfing, and jewelry shops, along with some restaurants, marked our way.

"We should talk with anyone who might look like they'd know Micah," said Tyler.

I was about to ask Tyler what that person would look like, when he stopped a few paces ahead of me, in front of a guy who looked to be in his early twenties, with stringy brown hair, a ratty red T-shirt, and cut-off jeans. He sat on the sidewalk next to a beat-up cardboard sign with the words NEED MONEY scrawled across it in black ink. Tyler reached inside his pocket and put a dollar on the small pile of loose change and dirty, crumpled bills.

I couldn't help staring at the guy's earlobes, which stretched around large black plugs that almost sank to his shoulders. I wondered how big the holes would be if he took them out. Piercings I could take, but plugs? No thanks.

Tattoos traveled up both of his skinny white arms like dead vines. His body moved back and forth in rhythm to music I assumed came from his headphones. It was hard for me to picture Micah hanging out with this guy.

Tyler bent down in front of him, and the guy removed one earpiece. "We're looking for someone."

"Oh yeah. Who?" The guy started flipping through songs on a small, lime-green iPod.

"Her brother." Tyler nodded in my direction.

The guy looked at me, beginning with my legs, progressing toward my face. His eyes spoke things I didn't want to hear. I instinctively wrapped my arms around my chest.

"What's his name?"

Even from where I stood, I imagined his breath stunk.

"Micah, Micah Stevens." I said his full name, and suddenly the heaviness of what we were doing bore down upon me.

"I don't know any Micah." The guy put his earpiece back in.

"Show him the picture," Tyler told me.

I held out the most recent picture I could find of Micah, the one taken at his last year's birthday dinner. The picture showed the two of us squeezed together in a large booth. Micah had on a black button-down shirt, his nicest one. His hair looked as if he had just woken up, but that's how he normally wore it, dirty and tousled, kind of like Tyler's, but not as straight. Dad had instructed us to smile, but my brother smiled only with his mouth. His amber-brown eyes looked like they were focused on another world.

Chapter Four

Crank. Ice. Chalk. Crystal. Speed. Trash. Tina. Tweak. Shards. The names of Crystal Methamphetamine. Poor Man's Cocaine. The last name scared me. Everyone knew cocaine could kill you.

After Googling it, I found a site that explained some of the common effects of using crystal meth. They were euphoria (lasting sometimes twelve hours), increased energy, weight loss, diarrhea and nausea, agitation, violence, and confusion. There was also increased libido, something to do with one's sex drive, meaning wanting lots of it. If Micah acted on that one, I didn't want to know. Chronic users often had drug cravings, depression, anxiety, and meth mouth, where their teeth rotted and disintegrated in their mouths. The worst were these intense hallucinations where users felt like bugs were crawling all over

"No." The guy spoke a little too loudly. "Don't know hin
started rocking back and forth again.

"All right, thanks, man." Tyler stood up.

I wanted to ask the guy to look at the picture again becau
had barely glanced at it, but Tyler had turned to go. I stuffe
picture into my back pocket, already weary. I wasn't prepare
the callousness, the apathy.

We were a couple of paces away when the guy shouted aft
"What makes you think he wants to be found?"

their skin. Bugs terrified me, so I was the most freaked out by that.

I scrolled down to a section about its effects on the brain. Meth released dopamine, the chemical that caused pleasure or euphoria. Over time, meth destroyed dopamine receptors, making it impossible for a person to feel good or happy on his own. It could take a whole year of being off the drug for the receptors to grow back, if they grew back at all. Users ended up requiring more and more of the drug so they could feel normal, because the drug changed the brain's ability to produce dopamine naturally. Meth addicts suffered from anhedonia—the inability to experience joy.

The last section of the site posted before and after pictures of meth users. They reminded me of those beauty-makeover TV shows where they showed the ugly picture of the person looking all sorry and somber alongside the pretty picture after she had her hair dyed and makeup applied correctly and was smiling. Only here these pictures were in reverse. A normal, happy-looking woman occupied the left side of the screen. The right side showed how she had been transformed into an older, thinner, almost unrecognizable version of herself, with sores on her face where she had tried picking at the imaginary bugs under her skin.

I stopped looking at the pictures. Micah was not like them. He didn't have sores or meth mouth. He was skinny, sure, but he had always been naturally skinny. "A regular beanpole," my dad used to call him. Micah looked like a normal, healthy eighteen-year-old. He was my brother. He knew joy. At least I thought he did.

Chapter Five

As Tyler and I continued toward the beach, I thought about what the loser with the huge plugs had said. *Of course* Micah wanted to be found. What kind of a person wanted to remain lost?

Tyler paused to talk to a guy and girl who looked more our age. He strummed a guitar and she sat with her knees up into her chest, painting her toenails a dark purple. Her short blond hair was matted against her scalp in thick chunks. Either she had used tons of product to get it that way or she was desperately in need of a shower.

Tyler asked if they knew Micah, and I showed them the picture. The guy continued to play a song in minor chords, which made the two of them seem even more pathetic. The girl looked at the photo with mild interest, yet said they didn't know him. She went back to painting her nails, but shifted her foot, knocking over the bottle, spilling purple onto their blanket.

We walked away before she could decide it was our fault.

"Those two weren't homeless," I said.

"Probably not."

"Neither was the guy before."

"Nope."

"Am I missing something? Is this the new rage? Pretend you're homeless to score a couple bucks?" It pissed me off. The inauthenticity of it.

Tyler shrugged. "Maybe they're bored."

"Then be bored. Don't pretend you're something you're not."

"Maybe they're protesting."

"With mp3s and iPods?"

He laughed. "The people gotta have their music."

"Look, Tyler, I'm sure you know what you're doing, but—"

"I know what I'm doing."

"Yes, but do you really think these people would know Micah? They don't seem his type."

Tyler stopped in front of a liquor store. "Maybe not the last two, but the first guy was high on something. I need a pack. You coming in?"

I shook my head. He went inside while I waited on the sidewalk. Though it was still early and overcast, I reached into my backpack and pulled out my sunscreen. I applied some on my face and arms. I could have used more color, but I tended to burn rather than tan. Micah was the opposite. Every summer his skin would get a nice golden brown.

Looking up and down the street, I decided Ocean Beach, at least the downtown section, was not what I considered beautiful. Everything was small and pushed together with no space to breathe. The buildings looked as if they needed a new paint job to cover the graffiti and to remind themselves of what color they were supposed to be. The cracked pavement collected scraps of paper and trash.

There was also a smell. It smelled like wet wool or stale bread. It smelled like a bad habit. I tried to make out the salty ocean water through the thick of it, but all I came up with was the smell of cat piss. But there was something else. Drugs. I could smell drugs everywhere.

I suddenly wondered if the person who had sent me the e-mail was secretly watching us and getting off on it. I had a sick feeling that it was all some big joke. Maybe there was no mystery person. Maybe it was someone from school, someone who wanted to hurt me. Keith's face cut through my thoughts. No, it wasn't his style. Total public humiliation, slander, cruelty, I had come to find that those were his weapons of choice.

He talks about you the most. That's got to mean something, right? If the person behind the e-mail was real, he could have at least told us where to find Micah. Although if Micah really was homeless, he'd probably be moving from place to place. Maybe he was crashing at someone's apartment or at a shelter, though I imagined him alone, curled into a ball on a cold cement sidewalk.

I should have come right away. Why did I wait? The answer buried itself deeper, which meant I wasn't ready for it.

Music played loudly next door at Hodad's, a restaurant claiming to have "The World's Best Burger! Under 99 billion sold!" Really? In OB? How did they know they made the world's best burger? What about China or Italy or even Canada? It looked cool inside, though. Old license plates from all over the country hung on the walls, and a line of people had already formed outside. Three men drank beers at the bar. They wore leather biker vests and their opened button-down shirts revealed bellies that hung over their waistbands. Old tattoos, symbols of their long-faded youth, stretched across skin that had expanded with age. This was probably why tattoos were best on leaner body parts, like ankles and feet. Their hair stood up straight in one-inch spikes. One woman stood next to them in a blue bikini top that barely held in her fake boobs. She threw her head back and laughed a little too loudly at something that had been said.

Two of the men looked in my direction. Trying to be polite, I smiled back through the window. One of them motioned for me to come over. Gross. I quickly dropped my eyes. I didn't have any daddy issues and wasn't about to give them the time of day. I wished Tyler would hurry.

A few moments later, Tyler emerged from the store and opened a pack of cigarettes. I waited while he removed one, watching his strange ritual. He licked both ends before he put the correct one in his mouth. It reminded me of old movies and how they were always tapping the cigarette against something. Everyone smoked in the black-and-whites. Katharine Hepburn always held a cigarette loosely in her painted fingertips. I couldn't imagine Bogart without a cigarette in *Casablanca*. Somehow it was sexy then.

Tyler lit his cigarette, took a puff, and released the smoke. I coughed. Today it wasn't so sexy.

"Sorry. Some habits are hard to break." He smiled, revealing his dimples again. I had never really noticed how great his smile was, which made me uneasy. I was a sucker for a great smile.

"Ready?" I asked.

I walked close to him as we passed Hodad's. One man whistled while the others laughed.

"Making friends?" Tyler asked.

"Shut up," I said. I wanted to get as far away from those men as I could. I felt dirty being there.

"Relax," he said. "You're stressing. You want?" He held out the cigarette between two fingers.

"I don't smoke." Which was partly a lie and partly true. I should have said I didn't smoke in public. I kept a pack of cigarettes in my top dresser drawer underneath my panties, and sometimes smoked late at night near the window in my bedroom when I was feeling rebellious.

"Too bad."

"I'm not planning to die of lung cancer when I'm forty-two." I said the words more harshly than I intended, and cringed inside. I could be such a hypocrite.

"You should do something to release all that tension. Why don't you go run a few blocks?" He chuckled. Removing his hat, Tyler ran his hands through his hair, then pulled his hat back on his head again.

I remained quiet. I didn't want to fight with him. The clouds didn't look as if they were going to break anytime soon, and the gloom dampened my mood, making it feel like the trip was going to be a lost cause. "Maybe this was a mistake." I tossed my empty coffee cup at a trash bin at the corner, but of course I missed, because I'm a terrible shot. I picked it up off the sidewalk and threw it angrily into the bin.

"Look. We have the whole day. It's beautiful out." Tyler looked up at the sky. "Well, it'll be beautiful once this burns off. It's supposed to be a perfect seventy-eight degrees. We'll take our time. Ask everyone we see. It'll be a good start."

"What if we don't find him?" I asked.

Tyler took another drag on his cigarette before answering. "The first time we came down here was sophomore year with Big Eddie and Sylvester. Remember those guys?"

I nodded, glad he was talking to me so I didn't have to obsess about Micah for a few moments. "Where are they now?"

"Sylvester's working at his dad's car shop. Don't know about Big Eddie. He's probably up the coast somewhere. Anyway, we had surfed all day by the pier." He pointed up ahead, and I could see the long, thin pier in the distance. "And the waves were totally going off. Micah was pissed because he hadn't caught one all morning. We all did, except him.

"Finally, I saw him up on a huge wave and about to go off the lip when *wham*! He ate it.

"We were like, 'Dude!' But he didn't come up right away. We had to pull him out of the water. He'd hit the floor and his forehead was bleeding."

Tyler paused to take another smoke. "Man, he was fearless. I'll always remember his stupid face, happy because he surfed so hard that his board broke in two."

"He was always getting hurt," I said. "Did he ever tell you how he got that chip on his front tooth?"

"Surfing, right?"

"No," I laughed, remembering. "He was in, like, fourth grade or something and out doing tricks on his bike. He was pretty good. We had this BMX track by our house where he used to practice. One day when he was coming home, there was this huge rottweiler. Micah's scared of dogs, so he was watching the dog and peddling as fast as he could to get away from it. He didn't see the parked car in front of him. He hit it and flew over the front end of his bike, landing face first on the asphalt. He came home crying with a bloody mouth."

"Ouch."

"He needed stitches and everything."

I laughed at the memory, but sobered up quickly, aware that Tyler and I were sifting through our memories of Micah, sharing bits and pieces, as if we were coming together to eulogize one already dead.

On our way to the ocean, we asked a couple more people if they knew Micah, and I was struck by how alike everyone looked: wrapped in dull, muted colors and dirt, stringy long hair or clumped dreads, discarded children of the 1960s flower people. Most of them carried backpacks or satchels, some of which were expensive brands. Many were musicians. Everyone smelled like pot. None of them was Micah.

The street ended and deposited itself into a large parking lot. Now it smelled of human urine, as if someone had marked his territory. I tried not to gag. To the right, another road led to the sand and a lifeguard station. Thankfully, Tyler headed in that direction.

The sandy part of the beach was smaller than I expected and only sprinkled with people. It wasn't the busy place I imagined it would become later in the day. Tyler took off his black Chuck Taylor's and started walking across the sand. I did the same with my flip-flops, holding them loosely in my left hand. The sand felt cool between my toes. I knew it would burn in the afternoon sun.

We walked by a man who lay on his back, covered with an old orange blanket. Next to him, a shopping cart and a beat-up bike stood guard. Shopping bags were tied to the handlebars, and the loose plastic rustled in the breeze. He stirred as if the wind had warned him of our presence. Then we carefully stepped around a couple of girls who were tanning. One lay on her back, the other on her front with her top untied so she wouldn't get lines. I had always wanted to do that. Tan lines were so annoying, but I never had the guts.

I wondered why Tyler was bringing us so far down the beach. It seemed to me that we'd have our best chances on the mainland, but I followed him to the break line, past the lifeguard station to where the water met the sand.

Tyler bent to roll up the bottoms of his jeans so they wouldn't get wet. I jumped back from the frigid water. It was definitely colder on the beach. My choice of a cute tank top and jean shorts now seemed a bad idea.

He looked over at the pier. "Guys are still out there." He meant the small showing of surfers clustered near the pier.

"He's not here," I said. I pulled my hoodie out of my backpack, put it on, and the inside instantly warmed my goose bumps. In the distance, the sun tried to break through the gray fog that still clouded the beach city.

"Well, he's not out surfing, but you didn't expect that, did you?" Tyler stood facing the ocean and closed his eyes.

I didn't know what to expect, I thought.

Movement caught my attention. A young woman sat digging in the sand with a little boy. She pointed toward the water, and the boy ran to the shoreline with a red bucket. He waited for the tide to come in, then scooped up some ocean and ran back to his mother, dumping the water into a large hole. The mother began molding the wet sand. I imagined it felt rough and cold in her fingers.

"He could be at this one place."

"Where?" I kept my eyes on the mother and child. The boy had ruined her sculpture by pushing it over with his hands. He jumped up and down, clearly excited by the destruction he had caused. Instead of getting angry, she smiled. Micah had loved to do that with my creations when we were kids, but after I'd had a good cry and he'd had a good laugh, he always helped me rebuild whatever it was.

"On the other side of the pier. It's where the—where certain types of people hang out."

The mother took the little boy's hands and pulled him into a bear hug.

"If that's where you think he'll be. We should check it out."

"I think you should be prepared." Tyler faced the ocean, and I had to lean in close to hear him over the sound of the waves.

"For what?" I followed his gaze out to the horizon and watched a wave form far offshore, and swell higher and higher, finally crashing into white foam.

"It's been a while. I don't know what shape he'll be in." Tyler squatted close to the sand. He took off his hat and shoved it into his back pocket. "Have you been around a lot of junkies?"

That wasn't the first time I had heard the term in regard to my brother. The first time was when my dad had caught him with a joint. My dad yelled at Micah, asking if he wanted to end up as some loser junkie. I've always wondered if Dad ever thought back to that moment and wished he could take the words away. Words stick, even when we don't want them to.

"No, have you?" I pictured the gaunt face of the meth addicts on the website I had found.

"He may not look or act like Micah anymore, is all. You need to prepare yourself."

What planet did Tyler think I lived on? Micah hadn't looked or acted like himself for months. There were times I'd thought an alien had entered his body and his mind was under siege, like *Invasion of the Body Snatchers* or something. I half expected to go into his room and find a pod or shed skin wadded up in the corner of his closet. What else could explain his silence? Screaming, "I hate you!" I could deal with, but indifference dug a crater between us and swallowed everything we once had.

Tyler turned toward me. "Let me do the talking. Keep your mouth shut unless I ask you to say something."

I looked at him like he was crazy.

"I don't mean to be harsh, but I'm serious." He gave me a look like I was a little kid who needed scolding. "You can't trust these people."

He said "these people" again, and it hurt to think that Micah was now included in a group I wasn't part of—that I wanted no part of.

I didn't protest. Tyler spoke as one in authority. As a general rule, I tended to submit to authority, at least outwardly. And it did feel good to have someone else taking charge. "Okay. You're in charge."

We left the shore and walked toward the tall pier. Most of the piers I'd been to were sturdy and wide enough for a car to drive down. This one looked frail, as if at any moment a large wave could come and smash it into the ocean. Out at the end stood a solitary white building with a blue CAFÉ sign.

I wanted to suggest we walk the pier, maybe Micah would be with the guys who were fishing, but Tyler headed under the pier, to the cement boardwalk by the parking lot.

We arrived at an old, dilapidated building. It looked like it had once been apartments, but now sagged empty, tagged in meaningless black scribbles. Two teenage guys sat in front of a thin, shirtless man like apprentices before a great bearded sage. One of the boys handed the man a cigarette. He took it and exhaled smoke that rose like incense above them.

Nearby, a woman with a large, professional-looking camera

pointed a long lens at a small band of surfers. She wore a string bikini top and cut-off jean shorts that barely covered her behind. Her deep cocoa skin, probably the result of hours of sunbathing, sparkled in the partial light. She nodded in our direction when we passed, but drew her attention back to the water as one of the surfers caught a wave.

I watched. In one fluid motion he was up on the board. He kept the top of his body low, almost hunched over, as he followed the curl of the wave. Spray trailed from his hand in the water. His feet moved quickly up and down the board.

Click click, click click, the woman's camera fired.

I imagined Micah on the board, but I knew it wasn't him. He talked a good game, but he had never been that good.

"You coming?" Tyler called from down a few steps on the path that led to a group of rocks.

Crossing the rocks proved more arduous than I expected. The water sprayed us as it came in with the tide. My foot slipped once, but Tyler caught my arm before I fell. He helped me the whole way across, and didn't let go until we reached the sand on the other side.

Right away, it felt different. There were no sunbathers or families, no volleyball games or flying kites. There was also no sand. Large, flat boulders with tide pools in between them separated the land from the water. If it were another day, I'd probably have wanted to explore and collect shells or something. Today I jumped over the pools without giving them a second glance.

Above, gray concrete buildings perched at the edge of a tall cliff and looked like one large jolt would send them tumbling into the sea. I stepped around a big lump of brown seaweed that sprawled on the rock as if it had crawled out of the ocean and died. Thousands of tiny gnats buzzed around it.

We approached a small group of kids who looked our age, huddling in a close circle in the sand. They were smoking pot.

"Hey," Tyler said.

A girl with long black dreadlocks and a bloodred hoodie smiled at Tyler and offered him a hit.

"Come on," Tyler said to me, and we walked around them.

"Don't you want to ask them?"

"They're too high. Waste of time."

Up ahead, a blue sleeping bag pushed itself against the base of the cliff. It moved a bit, and I thought I heard a moan. Through the opening at the top, I could see brown hair—Micah had brown hair. I had to check. Carefully, I walked across the rock, but the person's back was to me, so I had to bend down to get near.

"What are you doing?" Tyler called.

The guy rolled over. It wasn't Micah. He opened his mouth and two big holes stared at me where his front teeth should have been. His hand reached out to swat my leg.

"Get out of here! Ain't no show. Ain't no show unless someone's paying."

I backed away and almost slipped on the wet rock. Tyler caught me.

"Wait, don't go. I just need a little. Not much, just need some change, maybe a dollar or two. Pretty girl like you'd understand that."

"I'm . . . I'm sorry," I stammered.

The man struggled to sit up. The sleeping bag slouched to his waist, revealing his naked chest, gray like old meat. "Come on, man. You wake me up. You gotta pay."

"Let's go," Tyler whispered.

"I'm sorry. I thought you—" I said again.

"You gotta pay! You bitch!"

Tyler pulled me away while the man kept yelling, "You gotta pay!"

"I told you it's dangerous here." Tyler's voice was sharp. He led me back to the water's edge. Spray splashed over the rocks as the tide came in. "He could have had a knife or something."

I tried to pull away from him. "I'm not a baby, you know."

"Then don't act like one." He released my arm.

"I'm probably going to bruise." I rubbed the spot where he had held me.

"I'm sorry," he said, but his eyes still looked angry.

What's his deal?

"Are you all right?"

"Yes."

He glanced up the beach. "See that guy up ahead? He's a dealer. I want to talk with him. You ready to behave?"

Tyler spoke to me with that older-brother tone again, but I detected softness behind it, so I backed down.

"How do you know he's a dealer?"

"He just is."

I started to wonder how Tyler knew so much about this crowd. "You think he knows Micah?"

"Maybe."

We walked over to the man. He wore only board shorts; his muscular arms and chest were tan. A few tattoos covered his shoulders—one of a cougar, the other the face of a woman. He didn't look like a dealer to me, though I only knew what movies and TV had shown me: guys with goatees or mustaches wearing dark leather jackets who hung out in alleys and strip clubs, or stepped up to cars that then rolled down their windows. I didn't expect one to be out in the full daylight working on his tan.

"What can I do you for?" the man asked when we were in speaking distance. He flicked the last of his cigarette out onto a wet rock. The tiny embers continued to burn.

"Not buying today," Tyler said.

"That's what everyone says." He took off his sunglasses and looked directly at me. "How about you?"

I shook my head. He was older than us by only a little, though his eyes said he was ancient.

"Well then, I suggest you keep walking. I am a businessman." He put his glasses back on and turned his face toward the sea.

"Want to know if you've seen someone." Tyler held out his hand for the picture of Micah, and I gave it to him.

The guy ignored the photograph. Tyler reached into his pocket and pulled out a bill; I couldn't tell how much, but I knew it was more than a dollar. He gave it to the guy.

"Nice picture." His fingers touched the edges of Micah's face, covering me in the seat next to Micah. He handed it back to Tyler. "I've seen him around."

"You know where we can find him?" I asked.

Tyler shot me a look, but I didn't care.

"Did I say I was his personal babysitter?"

"We just want to know if he's okay." I felt my voice crack a little. I tried to make my face look concerned but tough.

The dealer looked at me for a few moments before he spoke. "What's he on?"

"Meth." I figured the truth was the best at this point.

He said, almost reluctantly, "I've seen him with a guitar, playing for money."

"Where?" I started to hope for a lead.

But he decided to give us a little lecture instead. "Everyone always thinks they can handle it, but they can't. Meth addicts are the worst. Start getting paranoid; losing their mind and shit, their teeth fall out."

He reached for a small tube of sunscreen that lay next to him and smeared it across his chest. For a guy who sold drugs for a living, I was surprised at how concerned he was about his body.

Tyler handed the picture back to me. I took the bottom of

my hoodie and cleaned the fingerprints from the faces.

"Do you know where he is?" I asked again.

"Let me give you some advice: forget about him." He lay back on the concrete and folded his arms underneath his head. "Go back the way you came. Give it another half hour," he said, jutting his chin toward the sky. "It's gonna be a beautiful day."

Chapter Six

Something like 80 percent of teenagers try some kind of drugs or alcohol before they leave high school. How the government came up with that statistic, I don't know. Maybe there were narcs or secret agents with clipboards at parties monitoring the exits, checking to see how many students were high when they left. Or maybe they got their information through random high school surveys, like the ones we had to take in health class sophomore year. The surveys that teachers tell you are "confidential" and "optional," but they make you take anyway. I remember filling that one out. My answers had all been no.

I had never tried drugs, not even marijuana. Not because of the lame celebrity antidrug marketing campaigns or the school's attempt at educating me, it was because I didn't like the feeling of being out of control. I drank a beer here and there at a party, but never more than one. People did stupid things when they were drunk. They said things they didn't really want to say and did things they didn't really want to do. They were annoying. I knew, because I was one of the only ones who wasn't drunk or high.

Jenn got herself date-raped at some guy's house last year when she was plastered. She didn't even know about it until the next day when she found some blood in her panties. I heard she cried about it because she had been saving herself for some football player.

After this one party, Keith and I had to give this guy who was too drunk a ride home. Less than five minutes in the back seat of Keith's blue Ford, and he announced that he had to throw up. Keith yelled at him to stick his head out the window. He did, but some of the vomit got inside the car. The next morning there was a streak of dried mustard-colored puke down both sides of the window. Even though I had helped Keith clean it with super strong, Pine-Sol–smelling stuff, every time I rode in his car I could still smell it.

If I had wanted to smoke pot, I knew exactly where to go. The potheads kind of stuck together in school, like every other high school group. They were mostly harmless. Pacifists. I didn't pay much attention to where the hard druggies hung out. But Micah knew. Somehow he knew.

I thought maybe I could keep my eyes open, watch him, see what shady people he hung out with. I never caught anything going down at school, but he didn't seem to have a problem finding the drugs.

Micah didn't know it, but I'd sneak into his room when he wasn't home. It wasn't hard to guess where he kept his stash. His Cali Girl guitar case always leaned against the wall in the same position, as if it lined up with some invisible mark on the wall. I would sit on his bed with the lights off and stare at the case.

Sometimes I'd open it and run my hands across the faded pink lining. I'd reach inside the compartment where he kept extra strings. Underneath spare picks, I could see the dirty white powdered crystals through the plastic wrap.

It was my way of keeping tabs on him. I always knew how much or how little he had been using by what I found in his case. It became an obsession of mine, though I made sure to put everything back exactly how I found it.

From what I could tell, Micah most likely snorted the crystals, which was probably why he had a chronic stuffy nose. Then he started smoking it.

Movies liked to hype smoking meth. There always seemed to be the gratuitous shot of the camera panning the drug lord's lair; his women sprawled on leather couches and shaggy rugs. The camera would then stop on someone taking a hit, where thick white smoke would creep out of her mouth and rise into the air like an angel.

I talked to Michelle about Micah, though she was better at commentary than listening.

"I bet something in Micah is predisposed to being an addict," she told me one day. "You know, kind of like the stuff we're learning in AP bio."

Interesting theory. Supposedly, certain illnesses run in families, like cancer, diabetes, even obesity. I wondered how disease started. What was the impetus? I mean, were cavemen sitting around discussing predisposed genetic disorders, like who was more prone to getting eaten by mammoths or by pterodactyls?

Disease, or the potential for disease, could be hereditary, so I decided to do a family tree of illnesses. I compiled a list.

My parents were both in good health. Since they were still in their forties, it was probably too early to detect anything, although I could tell by my dad's increasing waistline that he could have trouble with his weight in the future. My mom complained of occasional migraines, probably more due to stress than genes.

My paternal grandparents were both dead. My grandmother had died of lymphoid cancer. She felt sick for a while but didn't want to go to the doctor. By the time she did, the cancer had spread throughout her entire body. She died a month after her diagnosis.

My grandfather died three years later, after his third heart attack. He had been an alcoholic since he was eighteen years old, so his liver was also pretty shot.

I made a note on my list: the first signs of abusive behavior exhibited themselves with him.

On my maternal side, both of my grandparents were still alive.

My grandmother was in good health; however, she suffered from heart disease. She had a heart attack last year, but from what I have overheard from Mom's phone conversations, it sounded like she was doing well. My grandfather was healthy too, at least as far as I knew. His problem was being in a constant bad mood. He carried anger like a trophy. Most of us just laughed it off when the tension in the room started to thicken, but every now and then he'd whack you with it hard.

I made a couple more notes: anger, heart disease.

My mom had two brothers. One found out last year he had some kind of cancer. My other uncle was also an alcoholic. Currently, he was ten years sober.

More notes: cancer, alcoholism.

My dad had one sister who was on her fourth husband. The first two were supposedly abusive. Why she didn't stop after the first one, I don't know; maybe she felt she deserved it. Recently, a doctor had diagnosed her as clinically depressed and put her on medication.

Added to the chart: divorce, depression.

I didn't know much about the greats, except that one was an alcoholic, one was mentally ill, and one suffered from depression and anger. Lots of people in the extended family had some form of cancer. One cousin had a gambling problem and lost all of his family's savings. I had a second cousin who lived in Chicago and had that disease where you can't go outside, ever. Plenty of people were divorced and remarried.

After taking a brief inventory, I realized that I was doomed to inherit some negative trait, and I could see an emerging pattern of addiction.

Maybe scientists would find that addiction had a gene. It wasn't so far-fetched, and really, every human being could be a carrier. It seemed like most behaviors were already tied to one's DNA. There was the obesity gene, the depression gene, the antisocial gene, the greedy gene, the drug-addict gene, the "Oops, I didn't mean to kill my parents" gene, the child-molester gene, and so on.

We did this basic lesson in AP bio on heredity and eye color. Our teacher had us make out these charts with two parents' eye color, then we'd have to figure out the chances of the offspring having blue, brown, or hazel eyes. Brown was always dominant and blue was a recessive gene. Imagine if our teacher had us draw out a grid with all of our family's generational baggage? Who knew what was lurking in a person's DNA? Clearly, having children could be more hazardous than I had thought.

I watched this show once with a famous doctor who talked about addictions and how they were really diseases. He argued for the hereditary nature of addictions, which in my case meant that I should stay away from alcohol and drugs and gambling and food and sadness and stress.

Anyway, what I didn't like about the show was that he seemed to think an addict didn't have a choice in the matter. He said the addict suffered from a disease and should be treated like someone who needed to be in a hospital. He was speaking against the justice system in particular, and how so many addicts were locked up and treated as criminals, instead of the sick individuals they were. He advocated for better treatment programs.

Part of me grew angry as I watched the show. I could understand that once someone became a full-blown addict, overcome by their drug of choice, it had become a disease. Their brain chemistry even changed in some cases, like with meth users. They needed help. But calling it a disease or saying that addiction was based on predispositions or hereditary seemed to negate the personal choices it took for someone to become an addict.

To become addicted to something meant you had to choose that drug or that drink. Not just once, but many, many times. A person didn't become an addict after taking one hit, or every human being would be an addict of something.

Micah chose to do drugs even though he knew they were bad for him. He chose them over his friends. He chose them over his family. He chose them over his future. Not in just one moment, but in many moments. Every time he used, he chose death.

All of us are going to die. Jessica Slater, a girl from my history class, died last year in her sleep from a brain aneurysm. It could happen, anytime. But watching Micah slowly kill himself was too much. I hated it, and I hated how it made me start to hate him.

Why had he decided to take that path? Was it because of the

family history that lurked within both of us? Possibly. Was I destined to make the same choices? Maybe.

My dad had screamed at him one night, "Why? Why are you doing this to yourself? How can you do this to your mother? Don't you care about anything?"

Micah shut the door in my dad's face. Dad looked like he was about to tear it down, but he stopped himself, placed both hands on the door frame, and leaned his forehead against the door. He whispered something I couldn't hear. Then he pushed himself off and walked down the hallway toward his room and closed the door.

I remember watching the scene with my bedroom door cracked open and seeing the hallway between the two of them widen and expand, becoming a large chasm I was beginning to doubt could ever be crossed.

Chapter Seven

"I told you not to talk," Tyler said.

"He said he'd seen him around." I tried not to slip again on the wet rocks.

Tyler turned and faced me, right as the surf hit and sprayed, almost getting us. "The guy didn't know shit. He was just screwing with you."

"We don't know that for sure." My eyes started to moisten, and I pulled the hood of my sweatshirt over my head. "I'm fine." I matched his gaze. "We're fine."

"It's not fine! If anything happened to you . . ." He glared at me in a way that made me uncomfortable. "What would I do? Tell your parents they've lost another kid?" He started moving again.

"Sorry," I mumbled, following behind him. Tyler was right. I should have let him handle it. Who knew what that dealer could have done to me?

"Whatever."

Tyler stopped, and I almost ran into him. He took out another cigarette, lit it, and closed his eyes while he inhaled. "Let's go up there." He started climbing the steps that led to the pier.

The pier was wider than I had first thought and very sturdy. Out a little ways, it felt as if we were walking on the water. I could hear the waves breaking below. Their white foam peeked out at me from the spaces between the boards. About halfway down, Tyler stopped and leaned over the side of the rail that faced the surfers. I joined him and we both watched.

Three guys with black wetsuits sat equidistant from each other, their hands on their hips, still as a painting. They all looked in the same direction, toward a small ripple forming in the distance. Heading quickly from the shore, a fourth guy paddled toward them. As if there was some kind of understood respect, he stopped the same distance apart from the others and mirrored their stance on his board.

As the ripple grew and neared, one surfer came to life and began paddling toward the now expanding wave. No one challenged him; he would get there first. He got up on the wave in one motion, and twisted and turned with the water, riding it in. The other surfers watched him, but dropped their gaze before he finished, watching the horizon for the next ripple.

Micah had learned to surf when he was in junior high. During the summers, my parents lugged us to the beach every Saturday. Micah always begged for a better surfboard, and I secretly wished for thinner hips. I was in my shorts-over-the-bathing-suit stage, a little self-conscious about my body. It wasn't my fault that I had hit puberty early and had stupid Brad Billings snapping my bra strap during social studies.

While I anchored myself to a blanket, Micah surfed. He stayed in the water from the time we arrived until it was time to go. At first he wasn't any good. But he learned by watching the other surfers, and by eighth grade he could hold his own. When he could drive, I would tag along and lie out and read while he and his friends hit the waves. I didn't mind wiggling out of my shorts by then.

"Did Micah ever tell you the Boogie Board story?" I asked.

"No," Tyler said.

"It was when he was in eighth grade. He was out in the water on his board, like these guys." I motioned to the surfers below. "He's sitting there all cool—well, trying to be, because there were older kids around. My mom comes paddling out on her Boogie Board. Her hair's all wet and messed up. She's got raccoon eyes from her mascara running. There's a wave approaching, and my mom says to him, 'Come on, we can catch this one together.'"

I laughed, picturing the scene. "Micah totally ignored her. And my mom pretended like she made a mistake. She said, 'Oops, sorry. You looked like someone I know. My mistake,' and she paddled away. She overheard the guys saying, 'Dude, was that your mom?'

Micah told them he didn't know who she was, and they all laughed."

"Sounds like Micah," Tyler said, chuckling.

"I think Micah felt bad about it, because he always put his arm around her when she told the story."

"Micah liked to look cool." Tyler pushed himself off the pier's railing.

"He did." I realized we were talking about Micah in the past tense again. It scared me.

We walked to the café at the end of the pier. A CLOSED sign hung on the front door. Next to the restaurant was a small bait-and-tackle shop, also closed, with different sizes of fishing poles hanging in the window. I wondered if they had any of that fluorescent-colored bait my dad had gotten us while fishing in Mammoth one year on vacation.

Dad had bought fishing licenses and poles for the whole family so we could fish on the huge lake. Micah caught two trout, the rest of us nothing. At one point I thought I had something, and Micah came over to help me pull in the line, but we ended up with an empty hook, a tiny bit of fluorescent orange still hanging from the tip. Though I was bored most of the time, I liked throwing the line and sitting there in the quiet, waiting. The lake was ice cold, still, and dark.

"Micah never let us cuss around you, you know," Tyler said.

"Is that why he'd get all weird when I'd walk in on you guys during a practice?"

"Yeah. He'd say, 'Guys, not in front of my sister.' Like he was all protective of you."

"Like I've never cussed before." The truth was, I went through a cussing phase when I was a freshman. I spent the first two weeks of school adding "shit" and "asshole" and the occasional f-bomb to my vocab to establish my new identity. Micah frowned and told me to knock it off. I felt kind of cool at first, like I was playing a part, but it got tiring trying to be someone else. I guess that's why I stopped.

"I think he wanted to keep you safe. Like he knew you were special or something."

"It's impossible to keep someone safe."

Tyler and I reached the end, where a couple of older men were fishing. They sat in weathered beach chairs, the yellow nylon straps fraying at the ends. Their poles rested against the pier rail beside old five-gallon paint buckets. I looked inside one and saw the day's catch: two small gray fish.

A few paces ahead, another man started to clean a fish. Like an experienced surgeon, he spread out his knives on a newspaper. After choosing one, he stuck the knife in the fish and ripped through its belly in one cut. He reached inside, pulled the guts out, and deposited them on the paper. He dumped the gutted fish into the bucket to rinse it off. Before he began scaling it, he picked up a white towel, wiped the knife clean, then tossed the towel next to the fish's insides. I stared at the blood and guts, at the crumpled towel, and the awful stench of fish and rust and sweat turned my stomach. I felt sick.

"You okay?"

I nodded yes but wobbled toward the wooden railing. "I just need to clear my head a bit." I swallowed the bile that rose from my stomach.

Stop being such a wimp, I told myself. *It was a fish.*

But seeing and smelling the blood reminded me of when Keith and I were hanging out at CJ's house a couple of months ago. It was a spontaneous get-together because CJ's dad had restocked the garage fridge with beer and was away for the weekend. Parents were clueless sometimes. There were a handful of us, mainly the guys from the basketball team and their girls. Music played in one room, and a TV blasted ESPN in the den, where Keith and Josh were debating something about college teams and who would come out on top.

I couldn't have cared less. I opened the sliding glass door to the backyard to get some space.

Outside, the yellow pool lights set an eerie glow, so that's probably why I didn't see Charis, the point guard's on-and-off-again girl, in the lounge chair until I practically sat on her.

"Sorry. I didn't know anyone was here," I said. I knew who Charis was, of course, because she and I had been in the same math class all year.

"Oh!" She appeared startled. She sat up and began smoothing her brown hair so it fell over her shoulder in one long tail.

"Just getting some air. Cool pool," I said, not really sure how to engage in small talk. We had barely spoken a full sentence to each other. I sat toward the front of the class and she sat near the back.

"Yeah. It's new, I think." She slurred her words a bit and didn't look me directly in the eyes. A beer can lay on its side on the ground next to her.

"Looks it." An awkward silence followed. I became irritated because I really just wanted some time alone. "Well. Enjoy." I turned back toward the house.

"Rachel?"

"Yes?"

"I'm sorry, but I can't do this." She turned in the chair and placed her bare feet on the patio so that they faced my direction like a compass. "It's killing me, you know? I thought I could handle it, but I don't want to be this person." She moved her hair from one side to the other in a fluid sweep. "And seeing you in class every day—I thought it would be easier, but it's not."

Instinctively, I folded my arms across my chest, bracing myself for whatever she was planning to dump on me. I didn't want to know what she was talking about, but I asked, "What's going on?"

"We didn't do anything, really. Only made out and stuff. Just a couple of times. I had just broken up with Brian, and Keith said that you guys were going through something. But then I saw you together." She started to cry a bit. "I'm such a jerk. I didn't know, really. I thought he meant you guys had broken up. I'm so sorry."

I stared at the sky to avoid her eyes asking forgiveness. All I could see was black, as if the stars had gone into hiding.

"Are you going to say anything?" she asked.

It must feel good, I thought, *to dump your secrets. Quite cathartic, really.* I held my breath and exhaled very slowly. I wouldn't give her absolution. Somewhere in the back of my mind I thought only God could do that. "See you in class."

I was surprisingly calm as I walked back into the house. Keith sat next to Josh, watching the TV. They high-fived each other to something on the screen.

"I'm leaving," I said.

"What?" Keith asked. "Where you going?"

I shrugged. "Charis is outside. I think you guys know each other."

He stumbled to get up from his seat. He had been drinking, so he wasn't his usual smooth self. He looked at me like he was a scolded puppy complete with an expertly placed lopsided grin. Even drunk, he was good at manipulating people.

"Come on, baby. Don't leave. Let's talk."

I didn't want a public scene, so I headed for the front door. Then I realized we had taken Keith's car to CJ's. It would take me about a half an hour to walk home.

On the sidewalk, I thought about how stupid I was. How I was "that girl." The one whose boyfriend kept cheating on her. *Pathetic, sorry-ass girl. Everyone probably knew. What a joke.*

Keith called to me from the front door of the house, "Rachel. Where are you going?"

"Home." My legs felt tired already. *Could I even walk half an hour?*

He started down the steps, but slipped, his legs crumbling beneath him.

"Shit!"

I rushed to his fallen body, which was sprawled on the lawn.

"Shit," he said again, and turned his face up to me.

"Oh my God, Keith." Even though I was pissed, I was still compassionate. I bent to touch his face. Blood flowed from a large gash on the side of his head. He must have hit it on the corner of the stone steps. It scared me. All that blood.

"Don't leave," he mumbled.

"Shh," I said. "Let's get you inside." I bent down and, using my shoulder for leverage, helped him to his feet. Blood trickled down the side of his face.

Back inside, Josh and CJ helped me get Keith to the couch. CJ got a wet cloth and I held it to Keith's head. The others started to crowd around, but CJ made them back off.

"He didn't black out, did he?" CJ asked me.

I shook my head.

"Hey, man." CJ held two fingers in front of Keith's face. "How many fingers do I have?"

Keith tried to swat them away.

"He'll be fine," Josh said, after looking at the wound. "Head bleeds a lot." He revealed a faint scar on his temple. "I ran into a doorknob as a kid. It looks worse than it is."

By the time I went to the bathroom to clean myself up, I

looked like someone in a horror movie. Keith's blood had dried on my hands, the side of my face, and my shoulder. I was overwhelmed by this sweet, rusty-nail smell. I reached the toilet just in time to throw up.

"He's going to be all right," Tyler said, bringing me back to the pier and the reason we were here.

Tyler misinterpreted my silence, but I wasn't about to bring him into my personal business. As far as I was concerned, Keith was stuffed into the file in my head labeled Do Not Disturb. Maybe someday I'd be forced to open it up in future therapy sessions, but not today, not when I needed to be strong.

All of a sudden, the pier didn't feel very safe. If I wanted to, I could slip through the space between the rails and fall into the ocean, where I'd be swept away. Instead, I leaned on them and looked out to the sea. Tyler stood next to me, engrossed in his own thoughts.

The ocean gave the illusion of ending in a single line at the horizon, though I knew it continued beyond and beyond. The clouds didn't hang so low anymore, and sunlight hit the water, making diamond sparkles on the riffs and current.

"We'll find him," Tyler said.

I wasn't listening. The ocean moved thick like blood.

"Yeah, we'll find him."

Chapter Eight

Keith hadn't always been an asshole. He used to leave my favorite flowers, blue irises, on my doorstep late at night. Micah would roll his eyes and laugh at how "whipped" he was, but I didn't care. Keith pursued me, and even though the current version of the story told it the other way around, I knew the truth.

Keith asked me out sophomore year after a soccer game. We had stood just a little to the left of the concession stand. I was holding a Coke, and he had a hot dog with a thin line of mustard down the middle. He gave me that smile of his, which made me feel like I was being seen for the first time. I didn't even think about it. This was Keith Brandon. His physical attributes were already a given: white smile, brown eyes, deep voice, and great abs.

Keith was athletic, and anyone could see those abs in the parking lot after school. He'd always pull off his workout shirt and throw on the one he had worn earlier in the day before climbing into his car and driving away. I would come to find that he was also kind and funny, though maybe that was an act.

We were way casual at first. Talking on the phone. Eating lunch together on the quad. Walking to class. I couldn't go out on school nights, but we saw each other on weekends. We became one of those envied entities: a couple.

Micah didn't like Keith, but I didn't like every girl he dated either. He thought Keith was arrogant and acted as if he was better than he really was. Maybe Keith was cocky sometimes with the guys, but he wasn't with me. He was a perfect boyfriend: he held the door, waited for me after class, texted me when he'd be late, walked with his arm over my shoulder in that kind of possessive, but secure way.

I hadn't planned to sleep with Keith—it just sort of happened. He wasn't a jerk about it; the only comment he ever made was something about being on second base for a long time. He told me he liked dating a good girl. When he kissed me, it made me feel wanted and beautiful and hungry for more.

After we'd been together for a year, everyone assumed we had sex. I noticed that Keith never really corrected anyone on the matter. I think I got tired of all the pressure, and I just wanted to get it over with. I was going to have a first at some point, and I cared about Keith, so what was I waiting for? I knew it wouldn't be like the movies with music swelling in the background.

It wasn't that I didn't know about sex already. Micah and I had been given "the talk" when I was in the seventh grade. Dad started by saying that he knew we already knew about sex and that he didn't need to get into the particulars, though I hoped he would go into the particulars since I wasn't too sure what they were. He just wanted to ask us one question.

"Why buy a cow if you can get the milk for free?"

Micah and I looked at each other, then back at Dad.

"You get what I'm saying?"

Micah nodded, and I followed his lead.

"Good. That goes for both of you."

"If you ever have any questions, you can always come to us," Mom said. "We just wanted you to know that."

I wanted to know what cows had to do with sex, but I didn't say anything. Instead, I asked Micah later, and he told me it had to do with not putting out. I wanted to ask him about what that meant, but didn't want to show my ignorance. It didn't take long for me to learn all the coded language for sex. I was an astute listener and observer, and Michelle and I found a very informative site online. By the time I finished the eighth grade, I was up to speed on sexual innuendo and metaphors. Besides, there wasn't a day of school that passed without hearing some joke or seeing some public display of tongue.

But if I were going to give credit where it's due, I'd have to go back to the second grade and Greg Chase—the boy who told me that Santa Claus, the Easter Bunny, and the Tooth Fairy weren't real. I remember being so upset that I called him a liar in class. I went home and asked my mom if what he'd said was true. She told me that it wasn't. Santa Claus was real. The Tooth Fairy would come in the middle of the night and leave me money under my pillow in exchange for my teeth. And the Easter Bunny was the one who hid eggs for me to find. I was very relieved.

The next day I went back to class and confronted Greg, this time with the "my mom says" ammunition. Instead of refuting my mom, he changed the subject and told me where babies came from and what the dads did to the moms. I was shocked. My mom had always told us the stork story.

After school, I asked my mom about the babies. She told me that Greg was telling the truth and that she was sorry she had lied to me. She reluctantly told me the truth about Santa and the others.

"Does Micah know about Santa?" I asked.

"No. Do you think you can keep a secret?"

I said I could and suddenly felt very important, that she would ask that of me. I never told Micah. We set out cookies and milk for Santa all the way through junior high, though I think Micah had it all figured out by then.

By the time Keith and I were dating, I was a long way past believing in Santa and had learned that mystery and magic were reserved for very few things, including sex. There was this one night when Keith and I were at his house and his mom wasn't home. We were upstairs in his room, and I didn't stop it where I usually did. Keith kind of pulled away and looked at me like, "Are you sure?"

I closed my eyes and kissed him. It was over pretty quickly, and not as big a deal as I had thought it would be, which made me kind of sad. I didn't want Keith to know, though, so I smiled and acted like I was happy.

Big mistake.

Fast-forward to me dealing with Micah and drugs and rehab and finding out that Keith slept with Marcie, which I called the Marcie Armstrong Incident. Naming it had a way of providing distance. Keith told me he was sorry and promised he wouldn't do it again. I wanted to believe him, so I did. Another big mistake. After the Charis Incident, I told him it was over. I had some amount of self-respect.

The only person who knew about both Incidents was Michelle. Michelle had sworn to God that she wouldn't tell, which was huge for her. I suppose God knew already, and I was pretty certain he wouldn't be telling anyone. Micah and I were barely speaking to each other, so he had no clue. I just wanted it all to go away, to move on.

Turned out that Keith didn't feel the same. After his "accident" on CJ's steps, Keith went online, making our breakup instant public knowledge. In his manifesto, Keith spelled out how I came on to him, how I wasn't a good lay, how I was damaged goods, how he was glad to be rid of me, and how he was now open for business. He said it a bit differently, but that was the gist of it. Even though he lied, there was some truth to what he wrote—we did have sex. But he made it sound as if I slept around. In a million years, even after all the cheating he did, I would never have said those things about him.

Afterward, I felt eyes on me everywhere I went. I might have imagined it, but this was high school; that was how things usually went down. By the end of that first day back at school after the party, I felt sick, violated even. Girls looked at me with both shame and pity. A few even whispered, "I can't believe Keith did that," as I passed them between classes. It should have made me feel better, that not everyone would believe him, but it didn't. There was no use trying to counter Keith's account because he'd spoken first. Anything I said would just be interpreted as my trying to save face.

I confronted Keith in the parking lot after school, not caring who saw.

"Why?" I asked, walking up to him.

He leaned back against the hood of his car, shirtless. A small butterfly bandage covered what had been an open gash only two days before. He shrugged. "I was pissed."

"That's it?" I avoided looking at his familiar naked chest, and tried to find his eyes through the sunglasses he wore.

"You broke my heart. You really did." He took a breath and pushed himself off the car. "But I've got to move on, you know?" He reached into the open side window and took out a T-shirt. "Look, it'll blow over. If you want, I'll issue an apology or something."

"It'll blow over? It's out there." I made a motion with my hands that embraced the sky. "My reputation is online, it'll never be over." Once I said the words, I knew them to be true. I would be in college, and everyone here would still think of me as that girl who was easy. It would follow me everywhere. There would be no taking it back.

"Everyone knows people break up and get mad and say things they don't mean. God, Rach. You're so serious all the time."

"All that matters is perception." It's why my parents didn't see Micah for who he was becoming, and why I didn't see Keith for who he was.

A guy called to Keith from the gym building a few feet away.

"It was your idea to break up. But whatever, we can still be friends, all right?" He smiled his smile that won me in the first place.

"No, we're not friends. I don't think we ever were. Friends don't screw each other over." I turned and walked away.

I waited until Micah had come home from rehab to tell my

parents that Keith wouldn't be around anymore, that we had broken up. Mom said it was such a shame. Dad asked if I shouldn't think about trying to get back together with him. I probably should have told them everything, but they didn't seem to have enough emotional energy to deal with anything more. I wanted to be mad at them, but I couldn't. From their perspective Keith was gold, compared to Micah.

After telling them, I walked down the hall toward Micah's room, which stood at the top of the stairs. His face poked out of the small wedge between the door and the frame as I passed. He looked at me.

"What?" I said with a bit of a bite.

"He's an asshole," he said, then closed the door.

Takes one to know one, I thought.

Chapter Nine

We didn't have much time left on the parking meter, so Tyler thought we should get off the beach and walk up the opposite side of the street that we had come down. The wall of the boardwalk was busier now. Some people had the tourist look to them, with cameras at their waists. We avoided them and went directly to the ones who mattered.

We showed Micah's picture to two boys, both with long, beautiful blond hair.

"What'd he do?" the younger one asked me. His foot rested on his board, scraping it back and forth on the concrete.

"Nothing, we're just looking for him," I said.

"People usually do something to have someone come after them," he said boldly, and stared at me.

"We're not 'after him.' We just want to make sure he's okay. Look, do you know him or not?" My hands held my hips, and I tried giving them my most serious look.

"He's probably running from her," the other kid said, and they both laughed.

Before I could say something clever, they jumped on their boards and skated away. Their hair flew behind them as their wheels ground hard on the asphalt.

"Keep moving," Tyler said.

"They didn't have to be jerks about it."

"Whatever. They're just in junior high."

"Were you such a brat in junior high?"

"I don't know." Tyler smiled like he knew something. "You tell me."

I couldn't remember much of him from back then. "It's not like I hung out with Micah's friends."

"Yeah, you were kind of the bratty little sister."

"We're in the same grade. What, you're like a couple of months older?"

"Four."

"We're practically the same age." I was impressed, however, that he knew my birthday was in September. Only a few more weeks and I'd be seventeen.

"I'm still older," he said.

We entered a few of the stores: a used music shop, a surf place, a restaurant. No one had seen Micah, or if they had, they weren't saying anything.

At Galactic Comics, Tyler wanted to look around a little bit. The store smelled musty and felt claustrophobic, with tons of comics and gifts jammed inside. I picked up a Wonder Woman doll. Tyler grabbed Wolverine and karate-chopped her arm.

"Hey!" I made Wonder Woman take a swing, but she missed. "In real life, she'd totally kick Wolverine's butt!"

Tyler looked at me skeptically.

"Yeah, she'd lure him in with her hotness and that lasso thing."

"The lasso of truth?" His raised his left eyebrow at me.

"Whatever. She looks cooler. I love her red boots." I always wanted a pair of tall boots, but didn't have enough leg.

"But these yellow and black tights," he said, referring to Wolverine's clothes. "They're classic." He left me for another section.

I picked up a book with orange and black dots on the cover, and felt the smooth paper. I had a secret. Most of the time I chose books based on their covers. I knew I wasn't supposed to. Our librarian at school gave us the same spiel every year when our English class visited the library to learn the code of conduct and see all that the library had to offer. It was boring, but we looked forward to going because it meant a free period.

The librarian would tell us, "Now, you can't judge a book by its cover," and then she'd laugh. Our teacher, it didn't matter who, would always chuckle along with her, like it was some kind of lame insider teacher/librarian joke. I supposed it was true. Sometimes the cover didn't have anything to do with what was inside the book. But I didn't care. A cover helped set the mood.

My selection process was as follows: find a book with a cool cover, open it, read the first sentence. If I liked the first sentence, I'd flip to the middle and read a paragraph. If I liked that, I'd read the last sentence of the book. That's what usually sold me. I liked knowing where a story was going. And I loved happy endings. If the ending seemed overly sad and depressing, I passed.

Action heroes and women with very large breasts dominated the comics on the shelves. I recognized many of the popular superheroes. A whole section was reserved for Manga. This guy in one of my classes was obsessed with Manga. He had a new one practically every week. I couldn't really get into them because each one felt the same.

I looked at the cover of the book Tyler had in his hand. The character's face was drawn in charcoal and in shadow except for the whites of his eyes, drawing me in instantly.

"You read a lot of these?" I asked Tyler.

"Some. It's hard to keep up with so many coming out."

I pulled out a bright yellow one I recognized.

"A classic," Tyler said.

I shrugged. "I didn't get it."

"You read it?" Tyler sounded impressed.

"No. Saw the movie."

"Movies never do books justice."

I thought the same thing. Even with those Harry Potter movies. The cast was great and the special effects were good, but the books were always better.

"I didn't understand why the blue guy always had to be naked." I blushed a little. Tyler laughed. "Just because he's a mass of energy or whatever doesn't mean he can't cover it up sometimes."

I picked out another one because it depicted this beautiful woman with long dark hair blowing in the wind. I opened it to a random page and blushed again at the first image. Even in comics, people had sex.

"What's that?" Tyler asked.

"Nothing." I closed the book quickly. "When'd you get into comic books, or graphic novels or whatever they're called?"

"My dad. He's got this huge collection from when he was a kid." He put the book back and grabbed another one before revealing, "I've kind of got something in the works."

"Really?" I had no idea Tyler wrote comics. It made me wonder what else I didn't know about him.

"Nothing definitive. Just some storyboarding. Kind of an ancient-future thing."

"Like science fiction?"

"Sort of. More like Knights of the Round Table meets *Blade Runner*."

"So, something like this?" I picked up a Dark Tower book.

"Not really, but that series is awesome."

I flipped through some pages.

"Can I help you two find something?" the clerk called to us from where he sat in the front by the cash register.

"Just looking," Tyler said.

"What about this one?" I picked out another one I sort of recognized.

"Buffy the Vampire Slayer?" He laughed.

"Hey, don't knock Buffy. She's cool." Last year I was home sick from school, and I watched a couple of seasons online. Buffy and her hilarious Scooby gang helped me get through the flu. I loved how she didn't have it all together, but she still destroyed the Big Bad and saved the world, every time.

"Not really my style."

"What is your style?" I put Buffy back on the shelf.

"I'll show you sometime."

His promise lingered between us a moment before we left the store.

Next, we stopped at a beach clothing shop.

"Where's the bathroom?" Tyler asked the girl at the front counter.

The clerk pointed to the back of the store and Tyler followed his direction.

I approached the counter. It was getting both easier and harder to ask if anyone had seen Micah, easier because I had done it already, harder because each time someone shook his head, the discouragement stirred up more disappointment in my stomach.

"I was wondering if you've seen someone." I gave her the picture of my brother.

She looked at it briefly. "No." She returned the photo and continued reading her *Vogue*.

"Thank you." I put the photo back in my pocket.

Tyler returned from the bathroom with his Mao cap pulled low. He smiled encouragingly in my direction and I shook my head.

"My turn," I said, and headed to the bathroom.

The fluorescent lighting revealed more than I wanted to see in the mirror. My eyes looked tired. I let my brown hair down, tussled it a bit, and applied some lip gloss. I forced a smile. Better, though I didn't know why I cared. There was no one I needed to impress. Since it was beginning to warm up, I took off my hoodie and stuffed it into my bag. I turned to see the back of me in the mirror and decided I was more than acceptable. I looked cute.

"Let's try the hostel and then head over to the car," Tyler said when we were on the sidewalk again.

"Where's the hostel?"

He pointed up the street to a dirty white-and-blue building with a small wraparound porch. A college-aged girl with brown pigtails sat outside in a long flowered dress and white peasant shirt.

She was totally engrossed in whatever she was reading. Her legs dangled off the side of the porch railing. I kind of wished I could be doing the same thing.

On the front steps, a young man sat writing in a red notebook.

"Hey, man," Tyler said.

"Hey," he said, not looking up from his drawing.

"Want to know if you've seen someone." I held out the picture.

"No," he said, after looking at Micah, "but I just got here yesterday." He had some kind of accent, like he was from Europe or something. "You could try checking inside, but I don't know how much help they'll be. Most people keep to themselves."

The man at the front desk told us he hadn't seen Micah.

"The OB International Hostel isn't for street kids," he said. "You have to have a passport to stay here."

"Micah's not a street kid," I said. "He's—"

The guy didn't let me finish. "A runaway? You may have better luck with one of the homeless shelters in the area." He wrote down a couple of places and phone numbers on a yellow sticky sheet and handed it to me.

The girl reading outside didn't know Micah either. I was beginning to feel as if the trip had been pointless. The odds of finding Micah were, well, I didn't know. But if I were a betting person, I wouldn't even wager it. There were more people walking around than when we had first arrived, but I already knew that asking any of them would get us nowhere.

"You hungry?" Tyler asked me.

"I could eat," I said.

"It's been almost two hours. Let's move your car and get lunch."

We started toward the car and practically stumbled upon two men sitting on a blanket on the sidewalk. The older of the two had long gray hair tied back in a ponytail, and bony arms hanging out of a tank top that looked a couple of sizes too big for him. His companion was the opposite: heavy with clothes that didn't cover the skin peeking out of his shirt. These guys were authentic. In one morning I had become an expert in human profiling.

I handed the older man the picture when he asked for it. He looked at it for a long time. His friend next to him kept shaking his head while he picked at a scab above his right elbow.

"Does he have a tattoo?"

"Yeah, one on his arm," Tyler said.

The man nodded and gave me back the picture. I smoothed out the edge that had bent where he'd held it.

"He play guitar?"

"Yes," I said.

"What's his name?"

"Micah."

"Micah. 'Who is like God.' Hard name to live up to."

"Micah is nothing like God." I didn't have time for small talk.

Time was not on our side, but I tried patience. "Do you know where he is?"

"You spare a cig?"

Tyler handed him one and lit it for him.

"Can you tell us where we can find him?" Tyler asked again.

"Hard to tell. Hard to tell." The man smoked like he was eating his first meal of the day. "The wind. People move like the wind."

I sighed. The man was crazy. He probably should be in a mental institution.

"Jimmy would know," his friend suddenly said. "He's been here over thirty years." Blood oozed from his open scab, but he kept scratching at it.

"He looked good, real good. Maybe he'll be here today. You never know. You family?"

"Yes."

"Sometimes you got to give a person space. He'll come around."

I wondered why people felt they could give unsolicited advice. To tell the truth, I was getting tired of it. "How long did it take you to come around?"

He smiled without showing his teeth. "I'm taking my time."

"He doesn't know anything," I said to Tyler.

"No, he doesn't. Let's go."

"Okay. If you do actually see him, can you tell him his sister's looking for him?"

"What's your name?"

"Rachel."

"Come here." He motioned to me. Tyler moved nearer to me, but I gestured that it was all right. The man asked for my hand, and for some reason I gave it to him, as if it would be the most natural thing for him to read it and tell me my future. He drew a small heart with his finger in the middle of my palm and closed it with his calloused hand.

"Love. The most powerful drug of all."

I smiled at him. He dropped my hand, but I could still see the shape of the heart as if it had been tattooed.

"Thank you," I said, and meant it.

The man smiled at me as if I had made his day. Love. It was simple, really. That's all that mattered. It was what brought me here. It was what kept me looking for Micah.

We crossed the intersection, passed the coffee shop we had visited earlier in the day, and walked down the street toward my car. We had gone a few blocks before Tyler stopped.

"Does this feel right?" he asked, looking back the way we came.

"Umm. I don't know. Did we pass it?" I stood next to him, looking in the same direction.

"You don't remember?"

"I think it must be back there." I always had this problem. It took me forever to find my car after I had parked it. I usually asked whoever was in the car with me to remember. I had forgotten to ask Tyler that morning.

We turned around and walked back, but the car wasn't anywhere alongside the curb. I stopped again and walked back past the parked cars. Almost every meter was taken by someone else's car.

My heart started to race. "I know we parked on this side."

"You sure?" Tyler asked. He didn't follow me, but looked up and down both sides of the street.

"Yes," I said, though I was only, like, 70 percent sure.

I stopped in front of an empty space, and I suddenly felt sick. This was the spot. My car should have been right here.

"Try the alarm," Tyler called, jogging toward me.

I pushed the alarm button on my key chain a couple of times, pointing it in all directions. Nothing.

"I can't believe this. Are we that late? Did they tow it?"

Tyler stood next to me by the curb. He took out his iPhone to check the time. "No, we're still early."

"Someone stole my car. My parents are going to kill me." I sat on the curb and kicked an empty beer can out of the way. Tears began to form.

Tyler started dialing.

"Hello. I'd like to report a stolen car."

The police? I mouthed.

He nodded and gave the police the make and model, and the street we were on. He asked me for some information and was on the phone for a while before hanging up. "We can either wait for the police to come here and file a report, which could take forever, or go to the station, or go online."

I put my head in my hands. "Online? Aren't they going to put out an APB or something, whatever they call it? So they know what to look for?"

"Um, that would be in TV land. The guy on the phone said it could take a month to find the car."

"A month?" My voice wavered and I felt as if I were really going to cry.

"He said that Hondas get stolen for parts all the time, especially in this area."

"What am I going to do?" It was hopeless.

"Eat."

"Eat?"

"Yeah, you can use my phone to fill out the form." Tyler sat next to me and put his arm around my shoulders. I leaned into him, thankful for the comfort.

"My dad will be pissed when he finds out that I lied about coming here, and that I've lost the car."

After finding the car on craigslist, my father and I had driven an hour to check it out before we'd bought it from an older woman. Dad put up the cash, and I had a payment plan. After I gave him the first two payments, he cancelled the debt, saying that I had proven I could be responsible. He told me not to say anything to

Micah, but Micah told me later that Dad had done the same thing when he got his car the year before. Neither of us let on to Dad that we knew about the other.

"We won't call your dad. We can get someone else to pick us up."

"He'll notice I don't have my car anymore."

And he'll kill me, I thought. *Right after he kills me for being in San Diego in the first place.*

"Yeah, that may be a bit of a problem. You have insurance, right?"

"Of course."

Oh God. The insurance will go up.

"It should cover theft. You'll have time to come up with a really good story to tell your dad. Or work up the courage to tell him the truth."

I looked at him doubtfully. "I can't believe someone stole my car. It's not even that nice." Micah had always made fun of it by calling it an old lady's car—and it was. I'd gotten it from an old woman who had kept it in mint condition.

Tyler stood up. "It's been a shitty day."

I hobbled getting up, and he reached for my hand. He steadied me for the second time that day, and didn't let me fall.

Chapter Ten

Tyler paid for the pizza at the counter and carried the tray to a table by the window where I sat.

"Good thing you didn't leave everything in the car," he said, nodding toward my backpack. He took a huge bite of the pepperoni pizza. As he pulled away, a long string of cheese stretched between his mouth and the slice.

"Just my phone. I suppose that's not life-altering in the grand scheme of things." I pulled out my notebook and a pencil so I could write down the information from the police website that Tyler had found. I opened it to today's date before I remembered Tyler had left his backpack in my car. "I'm sorry about your backpack."

He shrugged. "I have my wallet and phone. No worries."

"You're so calm," I said. I took a few notes.

"Hmm?" He wiped the grease from the corners of his mouth.

"I can't handle it when things get too crazy, you know? Sorry about the reaction back there."

"What?"

"The tears."

"I didn't even notice. Besides, it wasn't my car." He took another large bite.

"True. But you could have freaked out. Now you're stranded here with me." I realized we hadn't figured out how to get home. "By the way, how are we getting home?"

"Already handled. Jones is free. He'll come when I call."

Mitch Jones was another friend of Micah's, one I didn't care for too much. He appointed himself the band's manager, and I guess he did a good job. They had gigs all the time. But I didn't like the way he looked at me and the way he smelled like BO.

"This webpage is so small. Not that I'm complaining." I was trying to make it bigger with my fingers. "And when did you get an iPhone?"

"Parents. Benefits of being the only child. You should eat." He pointed to the pizza.

I put down the phone and took a bite. "This is the best pizza in the world."

Tyler laughed. "You're hungry and it's the grease."

"What?" I said with my mouth full.

"From the pepperoni. Good stuff."

I took another bite, and some of the cheese slipped down the sides of my hand and onto the table. "Oops. Pizza is not great date food."

Tyler looked at me kind of funny. I turned my attention to the pizza while stuttering out, "I mean, not that this is a date or anything, but just a note for you and your future dates."

"Note taken." Tyler smiled with those dimples, and took a sip of his soda.

Tyler's smile was disarming, but I tensed, as if I had to be on guard. You never really knew what lurked behind a good smile. Some Shakespeare play I had to read for a class had a quote about that, something about a serpent's heart hid with a flowering face. Just because Keith had turned out to be a snake didn't mean every guy would be the same, right? I wondered how long it would take for me to be able to trust again.

I desperately wanted to change the subject. "If I haven't told you yet, thanks." I was grateful for his help. I hadn't known what to expect from the day, and Tyler's kindness was turning out to be unexpected for sure.

"For what?"

"I don't know." I kept my eyes on the food. "You're good in a crisis. You should be a fireman or something."

He laughed. "Yeah, a fireman."

"Yeah, like those hotshots, the ones who jump out of planes. Lola's dad used to be one."

"No way."

"You could do it."

"What part of someone jumping out of a plane into fire appeals to you?"

"I don't know. Saving things, like homes or people. It probably feels good helping people like that."

"I don't need to be anyone's personal savior. I'll leave that to someone else. You want a refill?" He was already on his feet and grabbing my nearly empty cup.

I watched him walk away and was glad that I hadn't come to Ocean Beach alone. Tyler stood with his back to me at the soda fountain, and I found myself checking out his broad shoulders. I imagined his lean muscles stretching across his back underneath his shirt, and remembered when he and Micah would practice in the garage in only low-riding shorts because of the heat. I shook my head to remove the image. This was Tyler, not someone to check out.

He turned, walked back, and grinned when he caught me looking at him. I felt stupid. Out of all Micah's friends, he was definitely the cutest. It didn't seem like he dated much, even though being in a band pretty much solidified that he could if he wanted to.

I took a drink from the cup he handed me. The Dr Pepper burned a little going down.

"So what do you want to do?" I asked.

"Right now? Finish this pizza." He reached across the table for another slice.

"No, I mean, you know, in your future."

"What is this? Twenty questions?"

"Maybe." I did ask a lot of questions—Michelle always told me that. But I figured if I wanted to know something, I should ask. I wasn't nosy; I was inquisitive.

"I don't know. College."

I looked at him kind of strange.

"What?"

"Nothing."

"Oh, just because I'm not in all those brain courses like you means I'm not going to college, right?" He looked out the window.

Surprised that I hurt his feelings, I said, "I didn't mean anything."

"Don't know yet." He turned his attention back to me. I was glad to see there wasn't any hardness in his eyes. "Maybe one of the JC's. Then I'll transfer."

"That's smart. It's cheaper that way."

"You sound like Mrs. Lopez." Mrs. Lopez was one of our guidance counselors who was good at her job. She really listened to you, like Tyler, actually. When Tyler spoke, he watched my eyes intently. He didn't look off to the side or down like most people did when they talked. He kept his gaze steady.

I blushed and picked up the iPhone again. I didn't understand why I was feeling so awkward. We'd spoken a million times before, but most of the time it was in passing. Just quick hellos and how-are-yous, never really face-to-face, alone.

"What about you?"

"I don't know either. I applied to a couple of places—San Diego, LA, Davis, some others. We'll see."

"One more year of high school."

One more year, I echoed in my mind. A year seemed like forever, but I knew it would go quickly. Then Michelle and I would be holding each other and sobbing at graduation like we had watched so many people do in the older classes. At this year's graduation, I hadn't really focused on the crying seniors. My eyes had been on the spot where Micah should have stood in line. Since our last name was Stevens, he should have been right between Sterol and Stewart.

"I wouldn't mind looking into some kind of graphic design," Tyler confided. "There are some art schools that look promising."

"That logo you did for the band was cool." When Micah had first shown me, it was so professional-looking that I thought he had hired someone. He told me Tyler did it, and I was surprised. I hadn't really thought of Tyler much beyond Micah's band and soccer season, where he was a forward for the school team.

"Here, give me that. I'll show you some stuff." He took his phone back and moved to sit beside me on the bench. His long fingers expertly slid icons across the screen.

"You have piano hands," I said.

"First instrument."

He pulled up his webpage, taking me through his drawings and designs.

"You're very talented," I said. "Did you do this in school?"

"Some in Mrs. Krell's class, but mostly on my own. It's kind of a secret, but she actually lets me run one of the Intro to Graphics classes."

Next to me, his arm leaned casually against mine. I didn't move away and neither did he. He felt warm, and I was suddenly very still.

"Micah never told me about this side of you."

"No, well, Micah only cared about the music." He showed me a sketch of their band. "I love to play, don't get me wrong, but I don't want to be stuck in a garage band the rest of my life. But it's cool for now."

"You guys have a great sound."

"Yeah, but without Micah . . ." His voice trailed off. "He was kind of the glue. We were supposed to take a trip this summer. Kind of like a graduation present for him."

"Where?"

"The plan was to drive down the coast of Mexico. Surf. Sleep wherever. Eat tacos off the side of the road. Try to get to my aunt's house."

"You should still do it sometime."

"I don't know. It'd be kind of a downer now. And summer's almost over. Here, let me help you fill out the form. I'll type in the information." His fingers quickly moved across the screen, much faster than mine had. "Okay. What's your license number?"

I reached into my backpack for my wallet and showed him my license. He laughed.

"What?"

"You look twelve."

"I do not," I protested, but I could see what he meant. My hair was pulled back into a ponytail, and I had this huge gaping smile, like I was a little kid going to Disneyland for the first time. My parents had overbooked that day, so Micah had to take me to the test. His only words of advice were to act like I knew what I was doing, even if I didn't. He had passed his test on the first try, so I felt the pressure.

Afterward, when I told Micah I'd passed, he hugged me and said he was glad because it meant he didn't have to drive me around anymore. He stood where I could see him when I got my license picture taken. He made some kind of crazy face, and I laughed right when the woman pressed the button.

Tyler and I finished the stolen car report and sent it. I crossed out the words "Fill out form" in my notebook.

"Hmm . . . I forgot about your list thing."

"I don't have a list thing." I crossed out "Search OB," and, inside, I started feeling better.

"When did you write, 'Fill out form?'"

"When we sat down to eat."

"See, a list thing. Don't you write things down even though you've already done them, and then cross them off, just to see that you've crossed something off your list?"

"Okay, psycho spy. I just like to feel productive."

Tyler laughed. "What else is on the list for today?" He grabbed my notebook and began reading. "Wake up and shower, crossed off. That's a good thing. Pick up Tyler. Check. Drive to OB. Done. Look around OB. Call Mom. Get gas. Not checked off. Hmm . . ."

"Give it back," I said, but I was laughing.

"Fill out form. Check status later." He flipped the page to the previous day and read the only words I had written: "Find Micah."

We both stopped laughing, but Tyler held my gaze and smiled encouragingly. I smiled too, because I felt that we were in this together. He gave me back my notebook.

"Thanks for helping me with the form. Getting my car stolen had better be worth it." Translation—we had better find Micah. "So, what do we do now?" I asked.

"Let me see that e-mail."

I pulled it out of my backpack and pushed it across the table.

"Too bad she doesn't give us an address or something."

I smiled thinking about how I had thought the same thing earlier. But something he'd said struck me. "You said 'she.' Why?"

"Just doesn't seem like a guy would go through the trouble. And this part, *He'd be upset if he knew I wrote you.* A guy wouldn't care about making another guy mad."

"I figured it was a guy, or someone making a joke."

"No, this isn't a joke." He folded the e-mail along the already worn crease and handed it back to me. "How long ago did you get this?"

"Two weeks or so."

"Micah could be anywhere, then." Tyler looked as if he were struggling to ask me something. "Why . . . never mind."

I looked down at my hands. I couldn't go there yet, couldn't deal with all the *whys* or *why nots*. It would have to be enough that I was looking for him today. It would have to count that I was trying to make up for what I had wished.

"You wanna keep going?"

I thought about what I'd have to face at home. The silence. The not knowing. The guilt. I was supposed to become a hero today. "Yes."

Tyler began texting and said, "Time for Phase Two."

"Phase Two?"

"Operation Dillon."

Chapter Eleven

Operation Dillon involved getting in touch with a surfing buddy of Micah and Tyler's. I thought about calling it OD for short, but I didn't, for obvious reasons.

"How do you know him?" I asked Tyler as we walked.

"We met surfing a couple of years ago. He's cool. We crashed a few times at his house."

"You think Micah could be staying with him?"

"Maybe. But Dillon's mom wouldn't like it."

"Why didn't we contact him in the first place?"

"Your e-mail said he was living on the streets, so that's where we started."

I didn't like the feeling that Tyler was keeping something from me, not lying necessarily, but feeding me the truth in pieces. "Is there anyone else we could meet up with while we're down here?"

"Dillon would know." Tyler stopped and turned to face me. "What's wrong?"

"Nothing." I looked down at the sidewalk.

"You're pouting." He let out a sigh.

I looked up. "Just don't sugarcoat anything."

This time his eyes avoided mine. "I won't."

Dillon Rodriguez lived in OB, not too far from the beach. It took us twenty minutes to walk to his house, a tiny duplex with a couple of bikes and an old rectangular trampoline in the front yard. Orange clay pots of red geraniums and cactuses led the way up the sidewalk to the red front door. A red door. I took that as a good sign. I loved red doors.

Dillon opened the door before Tyler could knock, and they were embracing in that sideways way guys do sometimes. A few things stood out to me. First, Dillon was short, not much taller than me, which made Tyler tower over him. Second, he was older, definitely out of high school.

"Tyler, *hermano*. Long time."

"Seriously. Couple months?"

"Probably. Who's this cutie?"

"Rachel Stevens. Micah's sister."

Dillon's brown eyes darkened at Micah's name, though it could have just been the shade from the yellow cowboy hat he wore. He tipped his hat toward me. "Pleasure. How is my buddy Micah?"

"We were hoping you could tell us," Tyler said.

Dillon leaned back against the door frame and crossed his arms. He seemed to be mulling over something, and after coming to a conclusion, he yelled out, "Ma!"

"What?" a woman's voice, loud and irritated, responded from somewhere inside.

"I'm going out."

"Where?"

"Out."

"Don't take the car."

"I gotta." He removed a pair of keys from his pocket.

"Put gas in it!" the woman shouted as Dillon shut the door behind him.

"Sorry about that. Mom's a little crazy. Tyler, you working out?" Dillon put Tyler in a headlock and practically wrestled him down the walkway.

Great, I thought, *he's one of those guys.*

He released Tyler and then flexed for us. "Pretty soon you'll be looking this good, right, Rachel?"

"Right. So have you seen Micah around?" I was beginning to get impatient with their male bonding.

Dillon stopped smiling. "She's kind of a killjoy, isn't she?"

I didn't wait for his answer. "Look, I don't mean to be anyone's buzzkill, but we're—I'm worried about Micah. I haven't seen him in months. The last I heard was that he could be down here. I think he's in trouble."

"Where have you looked?"

"Down by the beach, around the pier," Tyler said. "We heard he was sleeping on the streets."

Dillon nodded. "I'm not sure where he is." He took a cigarette from his back pocket and lit it. "He's pretty fucked up."

"How?" Tyler asked.

"Last time I saw him, he was tweaking pretty bad and all paranoid. He thought someone was after him." He looked away from me. "It was hard, you know, seeing him like that. He's a good guy, just, I don't know."

For a moment I thought maybe Dillon had sent the e-mail, but I decided he didn't seem the type. "*Was* someone after him?"

"Hard to tell. That shit he's on messes with your head." He paused and took a quick puff and exhaled, adding through the smoke, "He's a decent guy. I felt sorry for him."

Tyler looked away from me, took off his cap, and ran his fingers through his hair. "Well, do you know where we can find him?"

"I haven't seen him around here for a while, but I did see him a couple of weeks ago in Mission."

Mission Beach wasn't too far, the next beach north of OB—but definitely too far to walk.

"I don't know where he is, but I can help you look for him. If I were out there, I'd be glad to know that people were trying to find me. I was planning on heading to Mission anyway, if you want to follow my car. I have to stop to pick up my board at the shop. I'm pretty sure the owners knew Micah."

"Can you give us a ride?" Tyler asked.

"My car got stolen. Long story," I said before Dillon could ask.

"Sure. My ride's in the garage."

Dillon pushed a button on his key chain and the garage door slowly opened, revealing two vehicles inside. One was a white Toyota. The front end had a dent, and the mirror was missing on the driver's side. I was relieved when Dillon opened the door to the second car. It was old and black, probably from the '60s, and what I could only describe as beyond cool. It was the kind of car a greaser would be proud of. Her black paint reflected my face perfectly in the shine. The tan leather seats looked as if they were installed recently. No scratches, no marks of any kind defaced this car.

Tyler whistled.

"She's a beauty, isn't she?" Dillon admired her with us for a few seconds.

"This your mom's car?" I asked.

"Yeah, she's kind of punk rock that way."

I understood why she didn't want him to take it.

"Hop in."

Tyler opened the passenger door and climbed into the back so I could sit in the front.

I felt shy about sitting next to Dillon, but I knew Tyler was being thoughtful. "Thank you."

"Of course."

"And they say chivalry is dead," Dillon said, getting behind the dark wood steering wheel. He put the car in reverse and slowly backed out of the garage.

The car's engine roared as Dillon applied the gas. Instinctively, my hands reached for something to hold on to, but despite the loud noise, the car traveled smoothly along the asphalt. I relaxed into the soft leather.

At the first red light, Dillon pushed a button and the top of the car began to fold back, exposing us to the sun. He put his arm around the seat where I sat, the other hung over the outside of the car. People in the crosswalk turned to look at the car, and I could tell Dillon enjoyed the attention. He made an interesting picture: a short, stocky guy in a cowboy hat, T-shirt, and board shorts behind the wheel of a classic.

The light turned green. Dillon gunned the car again and she produced a low guttural moan. I heard Tyler say something behind me, but I couldn't understand him. We picked up speed. The wind whipped through my hair, and I couldn't help but smile as we drove toward the beach. I could see the water in the distance rising like a huge blue sun in front of us. For a moment I forgot about Micah. I thought about riding in that car and following the coastline to wherever it might lead us.

* * *

It led us to the first gas station.

After stopping, Dillon turned to me and held out his hand. I gave him some cash.

"In between jobs," he said, and exited the car to buy gas.

"I could have covered it," Tyler said.

"I know." I didn't expect Tyler to pay. Micah was my brother, my responsibility.

I relaxed and turned to look at myself in the rearview mirror. Not too bad. I wet my fingers and calmed a few of the windblown strands of my hair. I searched inside my backpack for my sunscreen.

"You want some?" I offered the tube to Tyler.

"Nah, I'm good. One of the benefits of being brown." To prove it to me, he held out one of his arms—tan and defined. Flustered again, I focused on applying a layer of sunscreen on my face and arms and legs.

"What's the deal with Dillon?" My eyes scanned the mini-mart where Dillon had gone to pay.

"What do you mean?"

"He seems like, I don't know . . ." My voice trailed off because I really didn't know. "He's older than us."

"Yeah, so?"

"So what does he do? Does he go to school? Does he work?"

"Dillon is classic. He's on the five-year junior college plan. You don't have to worry about him."

I watched Tyler for a few moments. The left side of his cheek gave no hint of the dimple it wore when he smiled. "I should call my mom, and make up some excuse about why I'm late. What did you tell your parents?"

Tyler shrugged. "I'm seventeen. What are they gonna do? Ground me?"

Mine would, I thought. I started fishing around in my backpack, forgetting for a moment that I had left my phone in the car. Tyler was way ahead of me. He held out his phone.

"Just tell them you're spending the night somewhere."

"How late do you think we'll get back?" I dialed Mom's cell.

"Better give yourself plenty of room," he said.

I hoped Mom's voice mail would pick up.

No such luck. "Hello?" she answered live.

"Hey, Mom."

"Oh, Rachel. I didn't recognize the caller." I heard the familiar sounds of her office in the background.

I winced, forgetting about caller ID. "Yeah, my phone died, I had to use Michelle's phone."

"How's shopping?"

"I found some shoes," I lied with practiced ease, adding, "on sale for only twenty."

"You and your shoes. Let's get rid of some of the old ones cluttering your closet. Just one sec, Rach." She spoke to someone else while I waited. "Sorry about that. What's up?"

"I wanted to see if it was okay to spend the night at Michelle's." I made my voice sound casual as if I didn't really care about the answer.

"Tonight? Don't we have something going on?"

"No."

"Wait. Yes, the Hammonds. They invited us for dinner."

Stay calm, I told myself. "Well, that's really more you and Dad, don't you think?"

"There's their son Jason. It would be nice of you to come for him."

"He's like, ten, Mom." I couldn't help the irritation in my voice.

"He's in the eighth grade."

Same difference, I thought. I tried a different tactic. "Well, I can make it if you really need me to. I was looking forward to spending some more time with Michelle before she leaves for her dad's. That's all." Michelle spent a couple of weeks every summer with her dad in Michigan.

A slight pause followed. My mom sighed. "Okay. You can spend the night. I know how much you'll miss Michelle when she's gone."

"Thanks, Mom." She was always a sucker for guilt. I hung up. "Your battery's almost dead." I gave Tyler back his phone.

"You're good," Tyler said.

I smiled, but inside I felt a little bad for lying. Maybe if I wasn't so good at hiding the truth, I wouldn't be here now.

Tyler sat forward and removed his sunglasses. "What do you want to do? You want to go?" His face was suddenly very close to mine. I backed away out of reflex.

"Go where?"

Dillon appeared at the passenger side of the car and lifted the gas pump off its hinge. He leaned his back against the car as the gas dispensed. His arms were thick with muscle and tats. Though I supposed a cowboy hat would look ridiculous on most people, he made it look cool.

"Hey, kids," he said.

"Hey," I said with a smile.

"You don't really look like Micah." He peered at me over the top of his sunglasses.

"They have the same color eyes," Tyler said from the back.

"Oh yeah? Brown?"

"Amber."

Tyler was right. Our eyes were kind of reddish brown. I kept my focus on Dillon and acted as if anyone would have noticed the subtle difference between brown and amber eyes.

"Were you guys close?" Dillon asked.

Were we close? The question echoed in my mind. Define close. I hated him, and he left without saying good-bye. "We didn't tell each other everything."

He nodded and said, "I have a little brother," as if that explained things.

"So what do you do, Dillon?" I asked, wanting to shift the conversation away from me and Micah.

"Well, I am currently working on a degree in business. I plan to graduate next year. For recreation, I surf, and I am a Leo. Anything else is top secret. I'd have to kill you."

I ignored the last part. "How old are you?"

"I'm finally legal, baby. Twenty-one. How old are you?"

"Almost seventeen. What kind of business do you want to do?"

"Finance."

"In this economy?"

"Money still rules the world."

"Why do you live at home?"

"Two words: free rent."

"Do you have a girlfriend?"

"Tyler, please make it stop!"

Tyler started laughing. I didn't see what was so funny. I genuinely wanted to know what kind of guy Dillon was. Was he the kind you blew off, or was there substance underneath?

"No more questions. I didn't agree to this torture." He finished at the pump, walked around to the driver's side, and got in. "Let's go see if we can find Micah."

Searching for Micah began with an anonymous e-mail, but it also came from a basic need. At first I needed to know that he was okay, that he was safe. But not only for him. Part guilt offering, my decision to find Micah was not entirely selfless. Micah was my only brother. It was as if some part of me were out there, lost and terribly sick. And I wanted to destroy the image of him sitting in our backyard shooting meth into his veins.

I was late for curfew. Michelle and I had taken in a last-minute movie. I sneaked in through the side gate and planned to use the back door. Tiptoeing along the pathway to the patio, I froze when I saw a silhouette. My first thought was that Dad was waiting up for me, but the body sitting in the chair was much leaner than Dad's. I almost whispered, "Micah," but something about his actions stopped me. His head was bent over his arm, and I watched him stick himself with a needle without even flinching. It didn't take long, a couple of seconds. When he finished, he leaned back into the chair and closed his eyes. I waited for him to move, but he didn't. He didn't even hear me as I crept past him and into the house.

In the kitchen I poured myself a glass of water and my hands shook. Some of the water spilled down my shirt as I took a drink. I was scared, more scared than I had been about anything before. But I was angry, too. It was the anger that stopped me from telling my parents. I left Micah outside, twitching and high, because I was pissed that he had left me, that he had decided to go somewhere I knew I could never follow.

Chapter Twelve

I had two high points my freshman year. The first was that I lettered in cross-country. The fact that we had only enough runners to field a varsity team didn't negate the accomplishment, in my opinion. The second was ninth-grade world history. About halfway through the year, right between WWI and WWII, our teacher decided to quit and move to Milwaukee. Instead of hiring another teacher, the school administration went cheap and got us a long-term sub.

The first thing everyone noticed about Mr. Parnell was his thick, bushy, red beard, the kind that looked like a mountain man's, the kind I wanted to shave off. After telling us a little bit about his life (as if we really cared about it), he confessed that teaching the next generation was a grave responsibility. I remembered that's exactly what he said, *grave responsibility*. I didn't know anyone who spoke like that except in old books.

The second day he divided us into teams and taught us how to play the game Risk—the one where the goal is "world domination." We played it every day for the rest of the year. At first it was pretty cool, but it soon became boring trying to take over the world all the time. None of us said anything to other teachers or our parents, though, because we never had homework and feared being called a rat.

Turns out, however, I did learn some interesting facts from Mr. Parnell. He was, after all, a WWII history buff.

One day, as I was just about ready to lay siege on France for the third time, something Mr. Parnell said caught my attention. It was in the early stages with Micah, when my parents still didn't know, and I was telling myself that everything was fine with him.

"How many of you have heard of crystal methamphetamine?"

I pretended to study the map of the world, though I knew it by heart from weeks of playing. If anything, I learned my geography from that class. A few people raised limp hands.

"Bet you didn't know how much it was used in World War Two. Variations of it were given to both Allies and Axis soldiers to help them battle fatigue. Soldiers who needed to stay awake all night or for days at a time took the drug. Supposedly, some of the Japanese kamikaze soldiers took meth right before they went on their suicide missions."

I had thought being a kamikaze had more to do with an honor code, but I didn't say anything. I squeezed one of my little purple infantrymen tightly in my fingers.

"Didn't it mess them up?" Ron asked from behind me.

"Sure. Soldiers came back totally addicted. Get this, even Hitler used it."

"No way," Ron said.

"Yes. He was a total hypochondriac."

"What's that?" Mike whispered next to me.

Someone who thinks they're sick all the time, you moron, I thought. I shrugged.

"He always thought he was going to catch something. He even thought the clean air could give him germs. He took all kinds of drugs. His doctor supposedly gave him daily injections of the drug for Parkinson's disease symptoms. It was considered a super drug, because it made you energetic and aggressive."

Hitler, a meth user. Kind of gave some perspective.

"Can't meth, like, kill you?" Keisha asked.

"Eventually. Look, meth has been used to treat all kinds of ailments, like narcolepsy and obesity. It's even used as a decongestant in Benzedrine. Legally, the drug companies now market meth under the name Desoxyn, which is prescribed for ADHD."

In one movement, every head in the class turned to look at Justin. He had been diagnosed with ADHD back in the third grade. He used to have to go to see the nurse every day after lunch to take his medication. He always came back super mellow.

He held up his hands. "I'm not a meth user!"

"Are you sure? You better read about what doctors are putting into you." Mr. Parnell laughed, which only made Justin madder. "Just kidding."

It was my turn to roll the dice. I looked at the board and debated attack; I decided to bide my time.

"All joking aside, crystal meth is very serious. I don't want to ever hear about any of you messing around with it." Every now and then Mr. Parnell's tone got all parental. "It will strip away everything you love, make you its bitch, and then kill you." Throwing in a cuss word really solidified that he was trying to make a point and identify with us.

The class became silent and we almost had a real moment. Until Ron yelled out, "Aw, he cares, he really, really cares!" Which made everyone laugh. Mr. Parnell got all flustered and ordered us back to world domination.

It was kind of ironic that we spent each day plotting different ways to kill and annihilate one another, especially since he had just talked about taking better care of ourselves. Imagining them all doped up on meth, I suddenly felt sorry for the little plastic men on the board. I put my head down on the table and surrendered for the day. Mr. Parnell didn't even notice.

I didn't think much about dying, although I almost did when I was in junior high. It had been raining for days, and at the first letup

Micah and I took out our bikes and went for a ride. The weather was perfectly crisp and a little windy, with large gray clouds hanging and swaying above us like clothes drying on a line. The sun played peekaboo, coming out for a few moments at a time before hiding again. We rode past the clubhouse and the school and out onto the dirt back roads.

I had to pedal hard to stay parallel with Micah, so I wouldn't fall behind and get hit in the face by the mud flying off his tires. The whole road had been transformed into a giant mud pit with small pools of quicksand and puddles of dirty brown water. My jeans were covered in thick splatters by the time we reached the drainpipes.

The two large concrete pipes ran underneath a major road, connecting to a concrete water channel. That day they were deserted. Usually you could find a handful of kids playing and hanging out there, especially in summer. And because of all the rain, they had a steady stream of water flowing out into the dirt passageway.

We parked our bikes on the side of the hill and ran down to the drains. I carefully avoided the water, while Micah splashed right through it.

"Hello!" he yelled into the dark drainpipe.

"Hello," it answered him back faintly.

Micah walked inside without having to duck his head.

"Where are you going?"

"The other side. Come on. I wanna see how full the river is."

The river, as we called it, wasn't really a river. It was a man-made channel where all the water collected during the rainy season. Sometimes it got pretty high, but most of the time it was bone dry and kids used it as a skate park.

I knew we weren't supposed to play in the drainpipes. Mom had told us this all the time, but I couldn't really remember why, so I followed Micah.

I walked behind him, straddling the stream of water, a foot on either side, and waddled my way through the tunnel. We had ridden or walked in the pipe before, just not when it was so wet. It was darker than usual because it was so overcast. I wished we had flashlights. I didn't like the idea of running into bugs or spiders.

"Isn't this supposed to be dangerous?"

"Look, we're almost at the end." Micah pointed ahead of him to the slant of light.

I heard a couple of cars pass overhead; their sound rumbled through the drain. I imagined a hole opening up and a car falling through it.

About halfway through the tunnel, I heard another noise, like a roaring during an earthquake. At first I thought it might be an earthquake, and I braced myself against one side.

Then Micah yelled, "Run!"

He bolted past me, back the way we came. I turned as well, but not before I saw a wall of water coming toward us.

The sound in the tunnel was so loud it felt like it had entered my brain and joined my racing heart and heavy breathing. I slipped and fell and got back up, but I had a shooting pain in my left ankle that traveled all the way up to my spine. I stumbled.

"Micah!"

The water was too fast. I knew I wouldn't make it. It felt like a cold, wet brick hit the back of my legs and knocked me down. I couldn't get back up. The water pushed me under along with tree branches, paper cups, cans, and mud. My arms and legs flailed all around, trying to find something secure to latch on to. I screamed, but my voice was swallowed by the noise of the floodwater. The water grew thicker with mud, making it almost impossible to hold my head above it. Something scraped my side and I was thrown against the wall and went under. I clawed myself out, coughing, trying to clear my lungs.

As I was about to go under again, someone grabbed my wrist and held on as the water and debris rushed past. Almost as quick as it came, the wall of water was gone.

I looked up and saw Micah. "You okay?" he asked.

"Yeah." I started coughing again and threw up.

Micah jumped off the metal ladder attached to the side of the drain, which he had climbed to get out of the flash flood. "Here, get on." He bent over and lifted me onto his back, carrying me piggyback out of the tunnel.

Outside, he set me down gently on the road and wiped my face with his hands and dirty shirt. My ankle throbbed and I couldn't put any pressure on it. I started to cry. I couldn't help it.

"It's okay, Rach."

"I did something to my ankle."

"Let me see."

Micah bent down and lifted up my pant leg. He touched my ankle.

"Don't! That hurts."

"It's pretty swollen."

I started shaking because of the pain and cold.

"I should ride home and get Mom."

"No, don't leave me here. What if it happens again?" I didn't feel safe anywhere near the pipes.

"Can you ride?"

"I don't think so."

Micah climbed up the side of the hill to where our bikes were. He chained them together and locked them. Then he came back down for me.

We were both wet and streaked with mud.

He bent down again in front of me. "Get on."

"You're gonna carry me?"

"It's not that far."

I knew it was probably a mile at least, but I got on Micah's back and wrapped my arms around his neck. He was bigger than me, but not by much, so I knew it would be hard for him to carry me all that way, not that he said anything.

"Mom's gonna kill me, and then you," I said.

"Nah. We'll just tell her you fell off your bike."

"How?"

"Your back tire slipped and spun in some mud, and then the whole thing flipped. I fell helping you up."

"Yeah, that's why we're so dirty."

"While she's checking out your ankle, I'll come back and get the bikes. She'll never know."

"You think it's broken?"

"Probably sprained."

Micah's breathing labored as he carried me. I tried not to move, to make it easier for him, and rested my head on his shoulder.

"Thanks for saving my life."

"That's what older brothers are for."

"If it had been you, I couldn't have held on for so long." There was no way I could have pulled him out of the flood.

"Yeah, I'd probably be dead by now." He tried to laugh, but he couldn't catch enough breath. "Nah, you would have found a way. If you had the chance, you would have saved me."

Chapter Thirteen

Mission Beach, another beach in San Diego County, was on a stretch of sandbar along the Pacific Ocean. Between Ocean and Mission Beach the coastline broke, creating an inlet of water that spilled into Mission Bay. The only way to access Mission Beach was to head inland by car and then over a long bridge that connected to it. The map looked confusing, and watching Dillon navigate the roads didn't provide any more clarity, but it didn't really matter; I was happy to be moving forward.

Once over the bridge, we could see the bay looping itself in and around the land, where hotels laid claim to pristine spots of sand. Grassy parks with picnic benches dotted the landscape. Children played on wooden swing sets. Boats with white sails were tied to wooden docks.

I closed my eyes and lifted my face to the sun. Perfect weather. If Michelle were with me, she would have remarked on the deliciousness of the day. She had a habit of saying that word a lot. *Delicious.* Everything was delicious to her. I had tried on the word, but for me it didn't have the right fit.

The Big Dipper, one of the oldest running oceanfront roller coasters, reared in front of us at an intersection. It looked unsteady, and for a moment I imagined the cars flying off the track and crashing below. The passengers would die screaming, in a rush of adrenaline. Not a bad way to go, I supposed. You would be with a group of people, some of them maybe even your friends. My great-grandmother died a year ago. She was old, alone, and in a dark hospital room that smelled of antiseptic and urine.

The faint screams of riders made me want to jump out of the car, have some fun, fade into the crowds of people. But the light turned green and Dillon gunned the car again, causing heads to turn, and made a right. He parked in front of a store called 360 Surf.

The door chimed as we walked inside. All kinds of beach gear and large surfboards were stacked against the walls, a row of skateboards and skateboard paraphernalia were off to the left, and wet suits and clothes occupied another aisle. A man with bleach-blond hair wearing board shorts and a graphic T greeted us.

"Dillon, what's going on?"

They gave each other that guy side-hug and handshake.

"Hey, Reeves. These are my friends, Tyler and Rachel."

"Hey," he said, and shook Tyler's hand, then mine. "You picking up your board?"

"Is she ready?"

"Good as new. I'll go get her." He walked to the back and disappeared behind a curtained door.

"Reeves is legit," Dillon said, as if I were waiting for his declaration. "He and his brother Spencer own the place."

Tyler walked over to a rack of hats and began trying them on. He made a funny face at me when he put on a pink snow-flaked ski cap with long sides that tied under the chin. He held out a skull beanie for me. I put it on.

"Not you."

"No?" I asked. "Because what you're wearing says Tyler all over it."

"What do you mean?" He laughed. He removed it and tried on a baseball cap. I put the beanie back and pulled on a floppy sun hat.

Not long afterward, Reeves returned with a surfboard and another man, who looked just like him. They both showed Dillon the board, and Dillon ran his hands along the sides.

"She looks great. Hi, Spencer."

"Dillon," Spencer said. He nodded a greeting in our direction.

"Told you," said Reeves. "Anything else you need?"

"Well, I'm looking for some information."

"Shoot."

"You know Micah Stevens?"

"Sure. Sure. The guitarist."

"This is his sister. She's looking for him."

Reeves and Spencer looked at me with that sad expression I'd come to expect.

"He came into the shop, what? A couple of weeks ago?"

"Yeah," agreed Spencer.

We always seemed to be a couple of weeks behind Micah. We were too late.

"He wanted to know if I could loan him some money. I know I probably shouldn't have, but I felt bad for the kid. He didn't look good," Reeves said, giving me the sad face again. "I gave him fifty bucks.

"He hadn't asked for money before. He wasn't the type, you know, he's not a mooch or anything. Haven't seen him since."

It was odd hearing them speak about Micah, as if they really knew him. For me, their version of Micah had never existed before today. Their Micah didn't quite seem real.

"Did he say what he needed the money for?" asked Tyler.

Reeves shook his head.

"For drugs, right?" I said.

"Probably," said Spencer, avoiding my eyes.

"You can shoot straight with her. It's her brother," Tyler said. "We came all the way down here looking for him."

Reeves started speaking slowly, as if every word counted. "I've been clean for two years now. Micah didn't really ask for our opinion, but we gave it to him. Nothing I could really do beyond that."

"He used to come in here from time to time with a guitar slung over his shoulder and show us a new song he was working on," Spencer added. "They were good."

"Did he tell you he took off?" I asked. "That he didn't even graduate?"

"No," Reeves said. "Micah is a good kid. Funny. Talented, but he's playing a dangerous game."

"No one starts out selling," Spencer said. "It just happens. You need the meth, the coke, whatever, more than anything. And then you're in the cycle."

"Selling?"

They all looked at me this time with pity, except for Tyler, who studied the floor.

"I'm sorry, honey," said Reeves. "I thought you knew."

"Did you know?" I asked Tyler.

Tyler looked at me. "Yeah."

My gut felt like it had been hit. "Keep going," I said to Reeves.

"That's it. End of story."

"What does that mean, selling? Are there dealers we could go to or other kids like him that sell? Who supplied him? Maybe they know where he is."

"Whoa," Dillon said. "You don't just walk up to a dealer and say, 'Excuse me, sir, but we'd like a record of your employees.'"

"Why not?"

"It's not like it's being broadcast. Everything's underground. Besides, the shit comes up from Mexico now," said Dillon.

"Or white trailer-trash desert people," Spencer added.

"These people aren't part of little street crews." Dillon leaned in close for effect. "If you cross them, they'll kill you, wrap you in a plastic bag, pour gasoline on it, and set it on fire."

"All right. Enough, Dillon," Tyler said.

"So you're saying Micah was in a Mexican gang?" I vaguely remembered news stories about the drug-cartel wars happening in Mexico and near the border. It seemed impossible that Micah could somehow be connected.

"No, of course not," said Reeves. "He was selling, that's all I know."

Spencer said the obvious: "Your brother is into some serious shit. There's no way around it."

He's in trouble, not the kind you can get out of so easily, if you know what I mean, the more serious shit, the kind where someone could get themselves hurt or . . . The words in the e-mail played in my mind. I thought of what could take the place at the end of those dots.

"How do you know he was dealing?"

"You just know."

I hadn't thought it could get any worse for Micah, but he'd just gone from an addict to a dealer in a matter of seconds. My mind spun at the implications. Arrest. Jail time. I pictured him sitting behind the glass, reaching for the phone so we could talk during visiting hours. At least I would know where he was.

"What if it was your brother?" I wanted them to put themselves in my place, to understand that Micah wasn't some typical sad story. He had family and people who cared about him, people who weren't going to let him destroy his life.

"He's in a bad place," said Reeves. "He may need to go through some stuff in order to come out the other side. I know it's hard. It sucks, and it's difficult for families, but he needs to surrender, you know? To try and stop controlling his life. To learn that there is a higher power and purpose for everything."

I recognized some of his language from the Twelve Steps of recovery that Micah had been given in rehab. I had memorized the steps from the pamphlet, which now sat in a drawer next to my bed.

"Were you an alcoholic?" I asked. "You said you've been clean."

"I have a sexual addiction. It's a little different, but it's basically the same idea when it comes to addiction."

"You're kidding, right?" But Reeves looked so serious that I wished I could take back my question.

"It almost ruined his marriage," Spencer said. "Look, the hardest thing is that, in the end, it's not really about you. It's about getting out of the way so Micah can find himself."

I wanted to smack Spencer and Reeves. They acted as if they

knew Micah better than I did after only a couple of months. They had no idea what he had put our family through. They had no idea what he had put me through. My pain was real and had everything to do with me.

"Thank you for explaining my place in the universe so clearly." I turned and headed for the door.

"Rachel—" Tyler began.

"No." I didn't even look back. I stopped Tyler with my hand. "You are not allowed to say anything." I tried to slam the door behind me, but it was on some hinge, so it closed slowly as the chime rang.

I stood on the sidewalk. In one direction were rows and rows of houses. In the other direction was the roller coaster. I started toward the screaming. I knew I was overreacting to their assessment of Micah, but I had to get out of there.

A few minutes later, Dillon's car pulled up alongside me.

"Where are you going?" Tyler asked.

Out of the corner of my eye, I saw him leaning out of the backseat with his arms folded over the side.

I ignored him.

"Come on, Rachel."

I kept walking.

"Look, you can be mad at me all you want, but I'm not letting you take off by yourself out here. And it's not gonna help us find him."

The car door opened and slammed shut, but I kept my gaze ahead. Dillon gunned the car. Tyler suddenly walked alongside me, keeping pace with my steps and silence. Tyler had let me down. I wondered what else he had kept from me.

"Is this a joke to you?"

"What? No. What are you talking about?"

"Taking me around today, seeing my reaction. Setting me up?"

"Rachel, I didn't know those guys."

I stopped and faced him. "Why did you even come today?"

Tyler looked angry, like he did down by the pier. "You asked me, remember?"

"You knew Micah was selling and you didn't tell me. Why?"

He lowered his voice. "I found out a couple of months ago, before he left. He told me he had it handled, that he was stopping. I should have told you, but I didn't want to worry you any more than you already were. I promised him I wouldn't say anything. That's got to count for something, right? I couldn't rat him out."

He talks about you all the time, that's got to count for something, right? I looked at Tyler, confused. Could he have sent the e-mail?

Tyler took out a cigarette, and this time I held out my hand for one. He gave it to me without question or comment.

Sometimes Micah and I shared a smoke on the roof of our house late at night. We'd pass the cigarette back and forth between us like words in a conversation. From a distance it might have looked like a small firefly darting back and forth. I'd always give him the last hit. When he'd finish, he'd flick the butt into our neighbors' yard, which pissed them off, but we didn't care. They had a mean little dog that barked like a rooster at the crack of dawn every morning. We considered it payback.

I placed the cigarette between my lips. Tyler leaned in close and lit the tip with his lighter. As I puffed, the embers caught the flame. The smoke tasted good in my mouth.

"Someone's been keeping secrets."

"You don't know everything about me." I cradled the cigarette between my pointer and middle finger.

"I can see that." He looked at me seriously, like he was going to ask me something, but he decided against it and remained silent.

We waited at an intersection for the light to turn green. I shifted my backpack to one side and hugged my free arm against my chest. I watched the familiar gray ash begin to form on the end, and I waited until the last possible moment to flick it.

"Here, let me take that," Tyler said, referring to my backpack. I gave it to him.

"How old were you when you started?" I asked Tyler. Green. We began to walk again.

He didn't hesitate. "Fifth grade."

"Fifth grade? Yeah, right."

"Truth. Mark Carter sneaked a pack from his dad and brought it over. We thought we were the shit, smoking in my room." He laughed. "We didn't even know what we were doing. Then we heard the front door opening, which meant my mom was home, so we freaked out and opened the window, turned on the fan, and put the lit cigarettes on the roof. I know, crazy. We could have burned the house down. My mom came in and asked what smelled funny. I told her we'd burnt some popcorn. She told me we didn't have any popcorn and sent Mark home. That night my dad made me smoke a half a pack while he watched."

"That sucks."

"I threw up. He told me that the next time I wanted to smoke, I should remember that moment."

"Obviously that didn't work."

"Nah, I just wasn't stupid enough to smoke them all at once or inside the house."

My smoking had increased after Keith and I broke up and then when Micah left. I smoked in my room late at night, by an open window, of course. Though thinking of Tyler's story, I wondered if my parents knew but didn't really want to deal with it.

I stopped and placed my hand on Tyler's chest, blocking him from moving forward.

"Okay. Is that it? I mean, is that everything?"

"What do you mean *everything*?"

"Everything about Micah. You're not keeping anything else from me?"

He cocked his head a bit to the side and half smiled. "No more secrets."

"No more secrets," I repeated. "Pinky swear." I lifted my hand.

Tyler didn't laugh. He crossed his heart and held out his pinky. I took it and we shook. It was a good gesture on both our parts, but I knew that neither of us could promise such a thing. No human being could.

Chapter Fourteen

When Micah entered the six-week rehab program, the people at the facility gave my parents a copy of the Twelve Steps for recovery. Micah was supposed to "work" the steps, which, from what I could tell, meant he was to take an honest assessment of his life.

The steps surprised me. The first one had to do with admitting you were out of control, because of the drugs or whatever addiction you had, and that you couldn't live life without help. The third step revealed that the help would come by giving your life over to a Higher Power or whatever you thought of as God.

The steps dealt with character, humility, and faith. I had expected them to be more psychobabble and scientific, not some kind of spiritual awakening. I wondered if Micah bought any of it.

He had never mentioned a Higher Power or God. I don't think he was much of a believer in anything except his music.

Step Number Two was about how believing in a Greater Power could restore sanity, which I understood because, really, Micah did become insane. That's the only way I could reconcile it in my mind. If you thought about it, most people suffered from some type of insanity at some point in their lives. And it was comforting to believe that there was a God or something bigger out there that could help reel you back in, that could help get you back to normal, whatever that was.

I never talked about it, but one time I actually thought I felt God. It happened the summer I went camping with Michelle and her family in the Sequoias, where there was nothing except miles of huge trees and rivers and waterfalls. We had camped along a river marked by large round boulders. We had two tents at the site, one for her parents and little brother, and the other just for Michelle and me.

The first night we grilled chicken kabobs over the fire and roasted marshmallows and made s'mores. Her parents always went all out, doing everything by the book, as if they had taken Camping 101. They even told us ghost stories around the campfire, something about a car and handprints on a foggy window. I didn't believe it; I had heard it before, but I gave them an A for effort.

That night, after everyone was asleep in their tents, I heard dragging footsteps outside. I froze in my sleeping bag, thinking it was a bear. I tried to remember what the pamphlet Michelle's father had picked up at the ranger station said about bears, something about how waving one's arms and making lots of noise would scare them away. I couldn't remember anything about what to do if they came to your tent. I stayed very still, trying not to make a sound with my breathing. Michelle snored softly. On the side of the tent, I saw a silhouette in the moonlight. It moved near the fire pit. I was convinced it was a medium-size bear, although it could have been a deer or a raccoon, or even a very large squirrel. The footsteps walked all the way around our tent and away from it. I was too scared to unzip the opening to see for sure and had a rough time sleeping for the rest of the night. As soon as a subtle light crept over the tent, I got out of my sleeping bag and slipped my running shoes over the socks I had slept in.

Cool air met my face when I left the tent. I zipped up my sweatshirt, pulled the hood over my head, and started to jog, following the line of the river. I loved early-morning runs. There was something special about getting up before everyone else, something magical about seeing the world as it opened its eyes. Everything was clean, in focus, and full of possibility.

A couple of boulders pressed together formed a narrow bridge across the river. I leaped across them, my feet barely resting on the smooth, wet stones. On the other side, I veered away from the stream and ventured deeper into the forest. Soon tall trees surrounded me.

I found what looked like a narrow path and chose it. My feet made barely any sound on the forest floor, padded from years of decaying vegetation. I could see some kind of a hill up ahead and decided that would become my goal. Since I wasn't used to running at such a high elevation, my breathing became loud. I sounded like one of those girls being chased through the woods in a scary movie.

I reached the top of the hill and bent over. My hands fell on my knees and supported the rest of my body. I watched my small bursts of breath rise into the chill of the morning. Looking below, I saw that the path lead into a field of deep green grass. I hadn't seen terrain like that in the mountains. Intrigued, I walked down the hill.

Trees surrounded the meadow, so it was cool and shaded, much like the rest of the forest. Soft beams of light shone between branches and trunks. I put my hand through one and actually felt heat. A tiny stream of water collected in the spot; where it came from, I didn't know. I walked as far as I could without getting my shoes wet and then stood still.

Because it was so early, or maybe because I was finally paying attention, my senses seemed heightened. Small blue dragonflies hovered and darted over the grass. Gnats collected by a felled tree, then flew away to another spot as one big swarm.

I closed my eyes and felt as if I were not alone. I opened my eyes and saw only trees and grass and muddy water. But I could still sense a presence, so I closed my eyes for a second time. From somewhere behind me came a light wind. I heard it playing on the leaves, moving slowly. The grass began to stir. The breeze came to me and moved through my hair. Small, invisible hands pressed themselves against my face, careful not to leave a mark, and then I felt it sweep past me, picking up speed. Opening my eyes, I watched the grass sway in front of me. The swarm of gnats trembled and hummed. The trees seemed to open their branches and embrace the wind. They shook. And then all was still again.

I felt as if I were in a holy place, like how I should feel in a cathedral. I didn't tell Michelle about it when I got back to the campsite. The moment was my private gift.

After that camping trip, I would sense things before they happened. Like the night Michelle rolled Kim's car. We had been coming home late from a friend's house and weren't even going that fast, but the car began to fishtail and Michelle lost control. We hit a bank and flipped three times. I remember it happening in slow motion. For some reason I knew we'd be fine, so I was completely calm as the car skidded to a stop on its roof.

Like the accident, I also knew that Micah had started using again a week after he left the rehab program, although that wasn't too hard to piece together. I had heard him again, late at night, through the thin wall.

My parents wanted so badly to believe that he was well. The day they picked him up, he walked through the front door, and I could read it in his eyes. He wasn't ready. Knowing the steps on the list, I don't think Micah had made it past number one. He hadn't given up control. He had gone to rehab because he was underage and my parents made him. I didn't know much about the program except that it was like a very expensive military boot camp. I would hear my parents discussing the cost in low murmurs after dinner. Insurance covered only the treatment of major illnesses and diseases, like the flu or leukemia. I guess they didn't consider drug addiction major.

I found the Twelve Steps online and printed out my own copy, calling them Micah's steps. I hid them in my top drawer, the same drawer where I later kept the anonymous e-mail. At night I had a little ritual: I would take the list out, unfold it, spread it before me, and read it before bed. After a while I could recite all twelve by memory. I whispered the words, careful that no one in the house heard me if they passed by the door.

Saying the steps reminded me of how my mom would have me repeat a prayer, one of the only ones she remembered from her childhood, when I was very little. It went like this,

> *"Now I lay me down to sleep.*
> *I pray the Lord my soul to keep.*
> *If I should die before I wake,*
> *I pray the Lord my soul to take."*

It was kind of a morbid prayer, thinking back on it now. Making a kid pray about her death before she slept seemed a bit extreme, but it had the opposite effect. The routine and familiarity comforted me.

Micah's steps became another prayer that I'd release each night into the universe, to God, to the Higher Power, whatever it was out there that could help me. The steps became my own personal creed, though I never struggled with addiction. I tried to say them as I imagined one would say a "Hail Mary" or an "Our Father," as if some kind of magic lay in the words themselves. I meditated and longed for that contact with God that the steps spoke of, so that Micah would come back, because really, part of his leaving was my fault anyway. I was the one who had wanted him gone in the first place. I would free the words and picture them floating away from me, drifting to Micah, wherever he was, and keeping him safe.

Chapter Fifteen

It was midafternoon and the boardwalk was beyond crowded with beachgoers. People played volleyball, calling for the ball and yelling when it went out of bounds. The girls on the court all wore bikinis and had lean, muscular bodies. As we passed, a girl threw the ball into the air for a jump serve. She grunted as she hit it, and the ball streaked over the net. Point.

Even though I had gotten over my junior high fear of wearing a bikini, I still was more of a tank or sports-bra type than a string bikini girl. Keith always said that I had nice legs, and I knew it was true because he obsessed over such things. I was athletic, but I didn't have the guts to play volleyball in a two-piece. Besides, volleyball players were always picking the bottoms out of their butts, even on national TV during tournaments. It didn't look comfortable to me.

On our right were triple-story beach homes; to our left, a low brick wall ran alongside the sand of the beach. All kinds of people sat on the wall, talking or watching the ocean. Many smoked cigarettes or drank from paper bags. Posted signs said no alcohol, though I guess that meant no visible alcohol.

Most of the guys who were drinking had the same look to them, shaved heads or short cuts, tatted up, and mainly white. They all seemed to belong to the same tribe, though none of them verbalized it. I wondered if Micah had a shaved head now. They leered as people passed by. I tensed, waiting for some kind of comment that never came. I just heard it in my mind.

When I was younger, I had a route I'd run on the weekends. It went through our neighborhood, past the skate park and the fields, to and through another neighborhood, and back again. One summer, construction teams tore up the fields. I had to run by the workers, and every time I did, I felt embarrassed because I could feel their eyes on me.

The guys on the wall were much the same. I thought about asking some of them about Micah but decided against it. There was an undercurrent to the place that the weather and water and sand could not cover, a pervading ugliness that beauty could not stain. Drugs. Sex. Homelessness. Poverty. Lust. I could touch the emptiness and pain; it was everywhere.

A young man in a button-down white shirt and red tie stood up on the wall and began speaking.

"God knows," he said. "You may not think He does, but He does. He knows all of your secrets. Your lies. Your thoughts. He knows about the time you stole or when you drank yourself senseless." Spots of perspiration formed on his brow, and when he raised his arms, yellow patches stained his underarms. "He sees everything. He knows your pain, your suffering. Can't run from God. Where you gonna go?" He asked those walking by and a few who had stopped to listen, though I felt as if he were talking to me. Did he know something I didn't?

"Nowhere!" a woman shouted back.

"Nowhere," the young man said, and continued talking about how everyone was a sinner and needed God.

Someone clapped his hands as we walked past.

"Thank you, brother," said the young man on the wall, misinterpreting the gesture.

"Let's sit here a minute." Tyler motioned to a bench not too far from the public restrooms. We sat down and he said, "You're quiet."

"What do you think about that?" I pointed to the man on the wall, now thankfully out of earshot. "Do you think he's crazy?"

"What, like do I believe in God and all of that?"

"Maybe."

He leaned back against the bench, put his arms behind his head, and faced the water. "I think too many people try to define things they don't understand. Look at the ocean out there. We barely know anything about it. What really lives in the deepest parts?

How can that guy stand up there and tell us what God thinks? He's only saying what he thinks God believes." Tyler paused for a couple of seconds. "God is beyond oceans."

"Wow," I said, after I was sure he was finished. "You're deep." I grinned at him. "Get it?"

"Oh, now you've got jokes."

"I can be funny."

He looked at me with one eyebrow raised. "Why do you ask?"

"I don't know. This place. This thing with Micah. Makes me wonder why God lets it happen. You'd think if there were a God, he'd get rid of all the stuff that sucks. You know, like evil and homelessness, and hunger and drugs and suffering in general."

"You forgot crappy food."

"And bad hair days and smog—"

"Fungus and hangnails."

"Gross, but yeah. He could make it perfect." I realized once I said it that I didn't even know what perfect would look like.

Though we weren't close to the water, the sound of an extra-large wave crashed through all the noise on the boardwalk.

"Where'd Dillon go?"

"He said he had to take care of some things. We'll meet up with him later."

"It's nice that he's helping us."

"Yeah, he's cool."

"You think Micah's really still here?"

"Maybe. What do you think? You're the one with women's intuition."

I smiled at that. "I can't tell."

At the outdoor showers near the restrooms, a mom held her kid under her arm like a football and washed the sand off the kid's naked body. The kid screamed in anger. I hated sand. It got everywhere and in everything.

A man wearing a red beret started to set up in front of us. He had all kinds of brooms in a large trash can, and he pulled them out, lining them up against the low brick wall. He invited those who were curious to form a semicircle around him. He threw some more sand on the boardwalk and then began pushing it around with one of the brooms. After a few seconds, I could see that he was creating a picture. He exchanged the larger broom for a smaller one, to create the detail of petals on the large flower he had sketched in the loose sand. The bristles of the broom marked long, thin lines so that the pavement showed through in places. He bent down, like a golfer examining his next shot. No one spoke in the surrounding crowd, waiting to see what he would do. He walked over to the wall and picked up another broom. This one he used to create the stem and a single leaf.

Tyler leaned in to speak to me. His cheek practically brushed against mine. "Weird," he whispered.

I was startled but said, "It's art," trying to ignore how close he was and how my body was suddenly very attracted to his.

"The guy is drawing a flower in sand." Tyler stayed in the same position. "It's stupidity."

"Well, he's not as talented as you, but he could be onto something: sidewalk sand art."

The man walked over to the wall and stood before the brooms. He hesitated, seeming unsure of what his next move would be. He chose the smallest broom.

"Sand castles are cooler."

"More work," I said.

"They last longer, though. My mom and I used to make those drip sand castles. You know, where you dig until you reach the water and then scoop out sand with your hand, letting it run down your fingertips and form globs, which you pile on top of each other."

"Yeah, I remember doing that. I liked trying to see how high I could make the towers." I nodded toward the sidewalk artist. "He draws a nice flower."

"As soon as he's gone, it'll get ruined," he said. "People will walk all over it."

"Not everything's meant to last forever." We watched the one flower slowly morph into a bouquet on the boardwalk's pavement. A girl talking on her phone walked by, oblivious to what was going on, and stepped on a leaf. There was a collective gasp.

"Sorry!" the girl yelled.

"You think I'm talented?" Tyler asked.

"You know you're talented."

"It means more if you say it," he said quietly, watching the artist work.

I thought about that and what it meant. "You're talented," I said.

The artist finished with one final swirl of the broom and bowed to the applauding crowd. A young boy who had been standing to the side of the artist walked around with an empty hat.

"Come on," Tyler said.

Before we left, I dug in my backpack and found some change. I dropped it into the hat.

"You want something?" Tyler asked, pointing to a snack and ice-cream shop.

"Yeah, an ice-cream cone."

Tyler and I stood in line behind a young couple who had their arms around each other. He had a hand in the back pocket of her shorts, and he leaned down and kissed the top of her head.

I remembered when Keith and I looked that happy—holding hands at school, watching movies, hanging out with friends—back when everything was simple and defined, back when I was blissfully unaware that he was sleeping with other girls. We didn't even talk anymore, which was strange at first because we used to talk or text every day. What he did made it easier to get over him, that's for sure, but it was still painful to know someone that well and then become total strangers. It made me afraid to get that close to someone again.

The couple in front of us ordered a single cone to share. I wanted to gag. Tyler asked me what flavor I wanted.

"Vanilla."

"Vanilla? No chocolate?" he asked.

"Nope. Vanilla's good."

"Okay. One plain vanilla," he said to the woman taking orders inside the booth. "I'll have strawberry and chocolate."

"Way to live on the wild side," I said.

"You have no idea," he replied, handing the woman money from the wallet in his back pocket. He gave me my cone first and then reached for his. He asked the woman if she'd seen Micah. She hadn't.

"Thanks." I licked the ice cream. It felt cold and good against my tongue. "You didn't have to pay for me. I mean, it's not like we're on a date or something." I immediately winced at having said the word "date" again.

"Who says I would pay for you on a date?" he said. We walked toward a large grassy area. On the lawn, people relaxed on blankets and chairs, and a couple of guys passed a Frisbee between them.

"You wouldn't pay for a girl on a date?" I asked him as we walked.

"Maybe not. Women are liberated today. They don't have to suffer from such inequality as to think they couldn't pay their own way." He licked the chocolate side of the cone, catching some before it ran over the edge.

"It depends on if you want a second date."

"You wouldn't go out with a guy again if he didn't foot the bill?" Tyler seemed genuinely surprised by the notion.

"I don't know." Keith had paid for me most of the time, but most of the time we didn't do anything that cost a lot of money. "It would bother me. There is an unspoken rule that the guy should pay, at least on the first date. If there are more dates after that, then I suppose he doesn't have to keep paying. Sometimes the girl could pay or they could go Dutch."

"I think it's a good test," he said.

"Test?"

"See if she really likes me or my money. If I don't pay the first time around, she won't be expecting it, so when I do pay, it comes from genuine desire, not obligation."

"That's the biggest cop-out I've ever heard."

"Why is it fair for the guy to always have to pay? Today both men and women work. Girls are flipping burgers alongside the guys. They should have the same opportunity to spend their money like a guy would."

"So has this little system of yours worked well?"

"What do you mean?"

"I mean, how many second dates have you had?" I reached out to poke him in the ribs.

"Enough." Tyler sidestepped my poke and finished his cone in one big bite.

"Hmm," I said. I still had half of mine left.

"Hmm?" he replied. "You doubt what I'm saying?"

"If you say it works, it works. I can't prove it otherwise, but you sound like you're evading the question. I asked you how many second dates you'd been on. You didn't give me a number." I enjoyed our pseudo argument. "I mean, what is 'enough?' Two? Five? One?"

"A couple."

"Again with the guessing." I smiled.

"How many dates did you go on last year?" he asked.

"I don't know," I said, which was the truth. What counted as a date when you were with someone for a whole year? Did hanging out at his house watching TV count? Or taking the car to the car wash? Or running errands with me for my mom?

"See!" He said it triumphantly, as if he had just made major points.

"It's hard to keep track when you're seeing someone." I regretted the words as soon as I said them because I had wanted to avoid the subject of Keith. I had been able to escape him practically all summer, but for some reason, Keith kept popping into my thoughts today, and now here he was between us. It was like a huge hose sucked the air out of our banter.

"Yeah, that's right. Keith. That was pretty shitty, what he did."

I shouldn't have been surprised. Of course everyone at school knew what Keith had said about me. I wondered if Tyler believed any of it. I didn't want to get into it and have to explain.

"Yeah, well . . ."

"Micah never really knew what you saw in Keith. He said he was the type of guy you generally wanted to beat the shit out of."

And so we were back to Micah again. For a moment I had forgotten why we were here, as if I were just strolling along a beach boardwalk with a cute guy who had bought me an ice-cream cone.

"Good thing he won't have to worry about that anymore," I said, and tossed the end of my cone into a trash can.

Chapter Sixteen

"Rachel."

I had kept my eyes closed.

"Rachel," Micah had whispered again.

I didn't want to look at him. I was afraid. Ever since he had come back from rehab, I had been waiting for something to happen, something to break again between us. I could sense him sitting on the floor by my bed. I pictured him holding his knees to his chest.

"You don't have to wake up." He waited. "I couldn't sleep."

I lay very still.

"It's weird being back. Everyone's walking on eggshells with me."

I barely breathed.

"You don't have to do that. You can, like, talk to me normal."

As if we ever talked anymore.

"I was going crazy in there. Those people. They're totally messed up. I know I've got some problems, but I can handle it now. I just needed some time away from everything."

He stopped talking. I heard him get up, but he didn't leave my room. I peeked at the clock—3:42 a.m.

"I know you're pissed at me," he said from across the room. He stood looking out the window. His silhouette cast a shadow on my wooden floor.

"I'm not pissed," I whispered.

"Yeah, you are."

"Whatever."

He was quiet. I waited, but the waiting got a little awkward.

Finally, Micah said something. "You should check out this moon, it's totally full."

Something inside me wanted to connect with him, to return to the way things used to be with us, so I pulled back the covers and joined him at the window.

The moon was huge and felt too close. It illuminated our backyard and cut through the night like sunlight, without the blinding brightness. Everything glowed in a soft bluish tint.

"Why can't you sleep?" I asked him.

"Too much on my mind."

"Like?"

"Lots of things." The words spilled from him. "The band. Writing new material. Returning to class. Graduating. Being stuck in this house. The future."

I put my hand on the glass. It was colder than I thought. Then I did something I hadn't done since we were kids. I put my lips up to the glass and blew a big fish face. I pulled away, and the window was all fogged up in that spot. I wrote my initials, RS, with my finger in the gray mist. Micah did the same thing, then wrote MS a little farther up the window.

"Are you afraid to go back to school?"

He sucked in his breath. "No. That's the least of my worries." He stepped away from the window. "So, we're cool, right?"

I shrugged. "Right."

"You know . . . ," he hesitated. "I'm still your big brother. If you ever need anything."

I nodded. I thought of what had happened with Keith. How if Micah had been more himself, maybe Keith wouldn't have got away with it.

"I'd better try and get some sleep," he said when I didn't say anything.

"You could try writing," I suggested.

He dipped his head down. "Nah, I think I've lost my muse."

"She'll come back."

"Maybe."

He closed my door behind him. I heard him enter his room

and shut his door. I turned back to the window. Our initials wobbled and ran down the glass. By morning they'd be gone. Smudges or streaks, the kind little children's fingers made, would be the only reminder that Micah and I had stood there together.

Chapter Seventeen

The afternoon sun tipped in the sky toward the horizon. Tyler and I were running out of time.

"Maybe you should call Jones," I said, stopping to lean against the railing of a ramp that led to a clothing shop.

"Is that the tone of defeat in your voice?" Tyler asked.

"Well, it's like trying to find Waldo or something. Even if Micah were here, it would take a miracle to find him."

"Don't you believe in miracles?" Tyler lit another cigarette. He must have been halfway through his pack already.

I shrugged. "My life hasn't been the most miracle-prone."

"Nope, they're rare." He blew a ring of smoke.

"You've seen miracles?"

"No, just one."

He took out his phone and dialed.

"You're not going to tell me?"

"I don't know if you're worthy." His eyes teased.

I didn't give him the enjoyment of a reply.

The door to the shop opened, and I moved aside as a couple of tall, skinny girls in extremely short shorts exited. Their long hair had been flat-ironed so it swayed as they walked. They each carried a small shopping bag. I saw Tyler follow them with his eyes. I thought, *I would never look like that. Not even if I starved myself.*

"He's not picking up." Tyler frowned. "Jones," he said into the phone. "It's Tyler. Give me a call when you get this." He hung up. "That's it. Phone's dead."

"There's always a pay phone."

"Do they still have those?"

"Somewhere." I looked around but didn't see any, and realized I had no idea where to find one. And I'd given all my change to the street artist. I guess we could call collect, but I didn't even know how to do that.

I was losing steam. Everyone had begun to blur together. I figured we should stop in the tattoo shop up ahead, but I didn't know if I could take it anymore. I felt guilty about being so weak. It hadn't even been a full twenty-four hours of searching, but I was emotionally exhausted.

"I'm tired," I whined, giving in to my fatigue.

"I have an idea," Tyler replied.

"What?"

"Come on." He grabbed my hand and pulled me with him.

I waited in line while Tyler purchased our tickets. He had insisted on paying again, and this time it really did feel like a date.

"Thank you," I said as he handed me the number of tickets I needed for the ride.

Tyler stood behind me; each hand held one side of the railing. I resisted the urge to lean back against him like couples did when they waited in lines at amusement parks.

Two little girls on the coaster screamed and screamed, and laughed in between their screams. I couldn't remember the last time I had yelled like that on a ride.

"Did Micah ever talk to you?" I asked. "I mean, like confide in you about his problems or what he was thinking?" Out of all of Micah's friends, he seemed the closest to Tyler.

Tyler leaned forward. "Your brother and me—wait, and *I*—"

"I'm not like that." I hated it when people did that around me just because I was in honors classes.

Tyler laughed. "Sure, you're not."

I started to protest, but he said, "Okay, okay, I was just kidding. Anyway, Micah and I had this, I don't know, this *thing* between us. I think Micah really got me, you know? He liked my art. We used to talk about real stuff, not just how hot some girl was or stupid shit.

"We had plans. We weren't going to stay, work our way up to manager at some place, get married, and pop out a few kids. We were going to, I don't know, change things." Tyler stopped as if he realized he'd given away too much of himself.

"How were you going to change things?"

Tyler shrugged. "I don't know. Through music, art, whatever."

"Sounds like a good idea."

"Last year Micah started becoming distant and paranoid. I knew it was the drugs. I called him on it. It's one thing to have a joint every now and then, but he was going way overkill. I mean he was using every week, sometimes a couple times a week. He'd come back high to class. Or he'd skip class altogether. Normally I don't have a problem with the occasional skippage, but Micah was cutting all the time. When I'd try talking to him, he'd tell me he didn't need another person on his case. He had it handled."

The line moved forward. We'd be in the next car.

"But I'd get these phone calls from him in the middle of the night. Sometimes I'd answer, but most of the time he left these crazy messages about how people were after him and his music, like the government or something. I mean, it was strange shit. He started doubting the band and questioning everything. He accused me of trying to take the band from him, like I wanted all the glory.

"One of the last practices he came to, he showed up late and high. We were jamming a little, just fooling around while we waited for him. He came in, screaming, and tried to hit me. I had to pin him down on the floor. Asshole, gave me a bloody lip." Tyler's hands went to his mouth as if it were still swollen.

"Sometimes I'd catch him sitting with his guitar and just staring. He wasn't strumming or anything, just staring. It was like he was gone. Like he wasn't Micah anymore."

"Micah hasn't been Micah for a long time," I said. I knew the look Tyler described. It was the look Micah had in the picture I carried in my pocket: dead.

"I tried talking to your dad once, but I don't think it came out right."

"What do you mean?" Tyler's talk had really woken my parents up to how bad things were.

"Let's just say your dad was in the 'looking to blame' phase."

"They don't blame you. They were hurt and angry. They got Micah into a program after your talk, not that the rehab helped."

"Most people need to go to rehab a couple of times before it really sticks. It took my dad three times."

I didn't know Tyler's dad had been in rehab. Micah had never said anything, and before today Tyler and I never had any significant conversation besides how the band sounded at a show or what movies we had seen lately. I waited for him to continue. It was clear a lot of pain lay behind his words.

"He used to be a drunk. He did the whole routine, binging on the weekends, yelling at my mom and me. He checked himself into a rehab program the day after he broke her favorite chair."

"How old were you?"

"The first time? Eight or so. It didn't really click for my dad until a couple of years ago when my mom threatened to leave him. I remember she had packed a suitcase for me. He's been sober going on three years now."

"Did Micah know?"

"Yeah, he's the only one I told."

Micah really listened and he was good at keeping secrets. He had had plenty of practice with me.

"Is that why you don't drink at parties?" Tyler was always the designated driver when he went out with Micah.

"Bingo." He motioned me forward and put his hands on my shoulders to guide me. "Our turn." I chose the middle of the coaster. I figured that would be the safest place.

"Have you ever been on the Big Dipper?"

"Nope," he said.

"Me neither. Here's to firsts." We high-fived each other.

The roller coaster took its time crawling up the first incline. I couldn't hear anything except the clicking and creaking of the old wooden track. At the top, there was a fantastic view of Mission Beach, but only for a moment before we dropped. I screamed. It felt so good to release all the day's tension. We sped up and down hills. There were no loops, but it was still fun. When we slid to a stop at the end of the ride, I tripped getting out of the seat and started laughing so hard that I had to bend over and catch my breath.

Tyler looked at me, and I said, "Bumper cars!" I took off running toward the sign. Tyler beat me to the entrance.

Tyler pretty much annihilated me in bumper cars. I blamed the little kids who wouldn't get out of my way, even though he somehow maneuvered around them with no problem. He kept slamming into the back of me. Maybe I really was a bad driver.

Afterward, I dragged Tyler into a henna shop. All kinds of designs covered the walls and the ceiling, but I already knew what I wanted. I pointed to a small butterfly. Girly and typical, I knew, but I loved butterflies.

I sat in a chair while a woman painted a blue and black butterfly on my outer left ankle. It only tickled; there would be no pain like a real tattoo. Tyler leaned against the wall and watched, but only for a few minutes. He cleared his throat and walked outside.

In AP bio, we watched a documentary that showed how a caterpillar became completely liquidated within the cocoon in order to reform into a butterfly. The caterpillar dissolved in slow motion, acid eating away at it, like it was stuck in some predator's stomach. The crazy part of it was that caterpillars did this over and over, made their cocoons, and transformed to become what they were born to be.

"What do you think?" I asked Tyler when I joined him later. I twisted my leg so he could see the henna.

"It's nice," he said. "You should get a real one. I'll warn you, though, it's addicting."

"That would be so permanent. What if I changed my mind?

If I'm lucky, this'll last up to four weeks." I caught a peek of the bottom of Tyler's tattoo on his arm. I reached out and rolled up his sleeve to get a better look. The eagle spanned the whole of his upper bicep. Black ink outlined the traditional Aztec drawing. It was clean, without color.

"Why did you choose this one?" I touched the top of the eagle and felt his muscle twitch.

"It's a symbol of courage and strength. The Aztec warriors used to paint it on themselves before they went to battle." He smiled ruefully. "Not much to do when you're stuck in Mexico for the summer. It also really pissed off my mom, which was another benefit."

I thought of the men painting this onto each other before battle, how Tyler and Micah could have been one of them. Tyler began flexing his muscle and the bird sort of danced. I laughed.

I hesitated, then said, "Can I ask you a question without you getting mad?"

"Sure."

"Why do you smoke pot? I mean, with your family's history. Maybe it isn't such a good idea."

"I used to smoke a lot, freshman year. If you want to get all shrink-like, maybe I'd say it was my coping mechanism. It helped take the edge off. I was really pissed all the time. Instead of dealing with it, I smoked. But then my dad started getting better, started dealing with his shit. He had these steps he had to do. One of the things he had to do was ask me to forgive him for everything he had put me through. He sat there across from me at the kitchen table and cried. I'd never seen him cry before. And I thought, he really means it. In that moment, I didn't want to hate him anymore. I wanted to believe him. Sometimes that's all it takes. So I forgave him. He stood up and hugged me, not one of our usual pats on the back, more like one of those bear hugs. He kept crying and thanking me for giving him another chance."

My eyes started to moisten as I pictured Tyler and his dad. I couldn't help but think about Micah and hope that one day that could be us. If Tyler noticed, he didn't say anything.

"Thanks for telling me. You never really know a person's story. Where they're at."

"I didn't want you to think that I was some stoner or something."

I gave him a sideways glance.

"I'm not saying I'm a saint or anything," he continued. "I really only smoke cigarettes now when I'm nervous or stressed out."

"You must be pretty stressed today."

Tyler smiled and his eyes had specks of gold with the green.

I broke his stare and turned my attention to the man selling peanuts and cotton candy. I wasn't ready for what Tyler's eyes said to me. We were here on a mission. I didn't want to get caught up in some side romance. Besides, this was Tyler. Micah's friend Tyler. If anything did happen, it could be complicated and messy. I didn't need complicated and messy in my life at the moment.

Out of the corner of my eye, I saw a quick flash of a guitar case. Brown shaggy hair. Skinny jeans and a black T-shirt. I snapped my head, but the guy had already been sucked into the crowd. I started moving toward the last place I had seen him.

"Rachel? Wait! What's going on?" Tyler called after me, but I didn't stop.

I pushed my way through the throngs of people.

"Micah!" I yelled.

Up ahead I could see the guitar case rounding a corner. I hurried, but when I reached the corner, he was gone. I grabbed a woman walking toward me.

"Did you see a guy with a guitar?"

She shook her head. I asked another person and another. No one had seen the guy with the guitar case. Maybe I had imagined him. Maybe I was crazy. Maybe.

Up ahead I saw the boardwalk, and I knew he'd be there. I ran again, looking all around. I heard him. I turned toward the sound of the guitar, anticipating the voice. He sat on the wall of the boardwalk, strumming. He opened his mouth and sang, and it was so beautiful that I began to cry.

"Rachel?" Tyler asked, coming up beside me.

I turned into him, and he held me as we listened to some boy I didn't know who sat on the wall. And I was sad because Micah's voice had never been that beautiful.

Chapter Eighteen

One night, not long after Micah had left, I couldn't sleep. Each time I turned to face the clock, only five small minutes had passed. It was 1:35 in the morning. Tired of staring at the ceiling, I decided maybe food would help.

As I walked down the stairs, a light was coming from the kitchen. My parents usually left one on to scare burglars away, but as I rounded the corner, I was surprised to find my mother sitting at the kitchen table. Her hair, normally neat, was pulled back into a messy ponytail, revealing the gray. She wore the same clothes she had worn to work; they were now tired and wrinkled.

She had photo albums scattered across the table in front of her. She rested the side of her head in one of her hands as she flipped through an album.

"Hey, Mom," I said, not wanting to startle her.

"Rachel?" She looked up at me, confused, as if she wasn't sure exactly where she was.

"Yes." I removed a bowl from the second shelf of the cupboard.

"It's late?" She said it like a question.

"Yeah," I answered her. "It's after one."

"Oh?" She turned back to what she was looking at, a page opened to our Grand Canyon vacation from when I was in elementary school.

I had begged my parents to go to the Grand Canyon after reading an old book of my mom's, *Brighty of the Grand Canyon*, about an orphaned donkey who navigates the canyon and the people he meets along the way. When we actually got to the canyon, I was disappointed because all we did was stand on top of a cliff and look out below. My dad was afraid of heights, so he didn't want us going anywhere near the edge. He wouldn't even let us take a donkey down the trail or hike into the canyon on foot.

In the album, our family stood with our backs against the protective railing and smiled, everyone except my dad. He looked nervously over his shoulder, so only the side of his face showed.

I opened another cupboard and found some granola. "You hungry, Mom?"

"No." She flipped through the pages, lingering every so often on certain photographs. Her free hand touched face after face on the page. I leaned against the counter, eating my cereal and watching her. I figured out the pattern pretty quickly. She stopped at all the photos of Micah.

I joined her at the table and opened another album. It was from when I was a baby, probably around one year old, so Micah was two or so. On the first page, my mom held me out toward the camera, my two chunky legs sticking out from under my white sundress. I looked like I was squealing with delight. Micah stood beside her, his face buried into her leg. My mom wore her hair in two long pigtails. She looked so young. So carefree.

"Rachel?" My mom said my name like she'd just noticed I was sitting next to her. "What are you doing up? It's so late."

"I couldn't sleep. And I saw the light on . . ." I let my voice trail off, figuring that would be enough of an explanation. Words had become quite sparse and unnecessary between us since Micah left. It was like part of her had left too.

She looked up from a picture of twelve-year-old Micah standing next to his surfboard. I remembered taking that one. "You have always been the good one, haven't you?" She reached out and laid her hand on mine. "My good girl." She turned back to the photograph of Micah. "He was still good here, don't you think?"

She paused. "I keep searching through these pages, wondering, where did we lose him? All I see is my baby's face. All I see is Micah."

I wanted to tell her everything, confess all that I knew about Micah. I wanted to tell her about how he'd started using a long time ago and how I had never said anything to her. I wanted to tell her about Keith. I wanted to tell her about all the times I had wished Micah would just go away, how I even prayed it because I hated him and because I hated that he was no longer the brother I knew. I wanted to tell her I wasn't always good.

I opened my mouth to speak, but she said, "Look, I know it's not fair for you to have to deal with this. I appreciate how strong you've been."

My eyes began to water. She patted my hand. "Shh. I know how worried you must be about Micah. We all are. Your father . . ." Her voice faltered. "We've got to think the best. He's going to be all right. You'll see. Everything will be fine."

I pulled my hand from under hers. "Yeah, he'll be fine." I ignored the words I wanted to say, like *I'm still here* and *I need you too,* and said instead, "He is going to come back any day now."

My mom turned her attention to the old photographs, back to the memory of a Micah already long gone.

"Any day now," she repeated.

I took another bite of the granola to help swallow the lie.

Chapter Nineteen

Tyler and I found Dillon's car in the parking lot next to a small stretch of grass. He sat in the backseat with his cowboy hat pulled down to cover his face. His arms hugged his chest. He looked so peaceful. I was amazed he could sleep with all the people passing by.

"Aw, look, honey, he's sleeping," Tyler said loudly next to the car.

Dillon stirred, tipped up his hat, and squinted at us. "Are you done with your little lovers' spat?"

I blushed. "I'm all right, thank you. Where's your board?"

"I dropped it off at home. I didn't want someone to steal it out here. Cost me a hundred bucks just to get it fixed, but that's okay because Reeves and Spencer saved her life." He climbed over the seat and slid behind the wheel.

"Couldn't you have gotten a new one?" I asked.

"That board and I have history. You don't just replace that."

Tyler opened the passenger door for me to get in.

"So where are we going?"

"I did some investigating of my own, put out a few calls, and I got us an address."

My heart quickened at the thought of an address. An address meant a location, a home, or at least a place where he had slept.

"Yeah, turns out our Micah was keeping some secrets. He had a sugar momma on the side."

"A girlfriend?" Tyler asked.

"Yep. Someone named Finn. She's a tattoo artist at a nearby shop. We're headed to her place."

Fifteen minutes later, Dillon parked along a street and we walked up an alleyway to Finn's apartment. Dillon rang the buzzer to the second floor. My hand rested against a wooden post, and I began picking off the old brown paint. I looked at Tyler and he offered me an encouraging smile, though his eyes were guarded. He put his hand on my shoulder and gave me a little squeeze. The gesture didn't comfort me, but I nodded and pretended that it did.

Dillon rang the buzzer a second time. The door could open at any minute. Any second now, and I could be standing face-to-face with Micah. What would I say? I should have rehearsed something.

How about, "You fucker!" No, too extreme. Not really me, just how I imagined I would be if I were a character in a movie.

How about, "You selfish jerk!" Better, but he might slam the door in my face. I guess I could simply say, "Hey," and see where it went from there.

Someone on the other side of the door unlatched locks and deadbolts. The door cracked open and an eye peeked out at us. My heart sank. It was blue. The door opened a little wider and the blue eye was framed by yellow hair. The eye scanned our faces and stopped on mine.

"Finn?" Dillon asked.

She nodded and opened the door. "He's not here." She turned away from us and walked up the stairs. Dillon, Tyler, and I exchanged a quizzical look, but I made the decision and followed.

Stepping into Finn's apartment felt like crossing into a different world. Long trains of red and purple fabric hung from the ceiling and ran down the walls. There were no couches, only large colored throw pillows and beanbags. Candles of all sizes and shapes had melted into every available counter and table.

Finn walked back to the stove. "Tea?" She poured some hot water into a cup.

"Sure," I said. "Guys?"

They nodded. I had to smile. I wondered if they had ever drunk tea in their life.

"You're Rachel. You look exactly the way he described you."

She set three filled cups on the bar, which jutted out from the kitchen. She walked around and sank into a green beanbag, crossing her legs in front of her. She wore a black tank top and matching leggings. Half of her blond hair was piled on top of her head; the other half hung loosely past her shoulders. A vine of roses and thorns climbed from her right wrist all the way to her collarbone.

"Can I see?" She pointed to Tyler's sleeve where part of his tattoo showed.

Tyler pulled up his shirt to show her.

"Good work. Most of those I see are pretty cheesy." She blew on her tea before taking a sip. "Know what it means?"

"Yes," he said, but didn't offer the meaning.

Dillon pulled up his shirt and turned around to show off one of his tattoos—his name in cursive along his waistline. "This was when I thought I was all gangster and shit. But this—" He rolled up one of his sleeves and revealed a large skull. It reminded me of the Pirates of the Caribbean ride at Disneyland. "*This* is what happens when you get shit-faced and wake up the next morning on a buddy's couch."

Finn smiled. "I've done a few of those."

"Maybe this was your work."

"Not my style. I would have added a yellow smiley face."

I sat on an orange pillow and studied Finn above the rim of the cup. She was older than Micah, more like Dillon's age. She was thin, too thin, just like those girls in Micah's rehab. But she was beautiful in a natural, no-makeup kind of way, not even mascara. She looked like the type of girl Micah would date. And then I knew.

"You said Micah wasn't here," I said.

"He left a couple of weeks ago."

If only I hadn't waited so long to come.

"Any idea where he went?" Tyler asked.

"Nope." She put her cup on the floor. "Most of his stuff is gone, but he did leave a few things." She gestured toward a room. "They're in the back corner of the bedroom if you want to take a look."

I got up and walked to the room. A queen-size mattress lay on the floor, next to a red lamp. A tall brown dresser with a vase of dead roses stood in the corner. Next to it was a black trash bag. I sat down on the bed and opened the bag, dumping the contents onto the floor: a pair of jeans, three socks, a guitar pick, a black cap, a broken pair of sunglasses, and *The Hobbit*. Of all my books, he'd stolen that one. I hadn't even noticed. I studied the contents of the bag as if they were a trail of clues Micah had left for me to follow. Why else would he have left the book?

I looked through the jean pockets. There was a crumpled dollar and a receipt for Chinese food in a front pocket. In the back, I pulled out a small white piece of paper with a telephone number scrawled in pencil. I stuffed the paper with the number and the dollar into my own pocket.

I stood up and surveyed the room again. Even with the window partially open, the room smelled sickly sweet, but it also smelled faintly like Micah. The flowers were shriveled and sat in yellowish-brown water. I wondered if Micah had given them to Finn. Was that why she'd kept them?

A small bookshelf held old magazines and art books. I pulled one out and was surprised to find *The Secret* lying on its side. It made me think that maybe I hadn't had enough positive thoughts about Micah. Maybe if I visualized finding him, we would.

I sighed. There was nothing here. Nothing that would lead me to Micah.

I tried picturing him in the room. His amp would have been plugged into the outlet with the light. He'd sit on the bed and play his guitar. I could almost see him, hunched over, concentrating.

I closed my eyes and tried to hear his voice, but I heard only the silence of the room and the murmur of voices in the other room. I couldn't hear Micah, and the fear that I had been evading found me: I'd forgotten the sound of his voice.

Tyler cleared his throat behind me. "You find anything?"

I pointed to the junk on the mattress.

"Hmm. Not very interesting prospects."

"No." I felt despair creep over me along with the familiar guilt. "Tyler, I think I blew it. I think if I had acted right away, if I had come down here right when I'd gotten the e-mail, I wouldn't be staring at an empty room. Micah would have been here."

"Yeah, he probably would have."

I turned toward him, surprised.

"You said not to sugarcoat anything." Tyler walked over to the bed and picked up the guitar pick. "Or maybe he wouldn't. Life's not determined by 'probablys' and 'would haves.'"

The way Tyler said things made sense, even when it was hard to hear. "What's Finn like?" I asked.

"She's his usual type. Skinny. Pretty."

I nodded. "She's an addict." I had intended it as a question.

"Yeah, I'm pretty sure that's how they met." He paused. "Come on, we should save her from Dillon. He'll be asking her out any second now."

"Find what you're looking for?" Finn asked when we walked back into the living room.

"Not really. How long have you known Micah?" This time I opted for a thick black beanbag.

Dillon interrupted, "Time for a smoke," and stood up. "Tyler?"

Tyler looked at me as if to make sure I'd be all right.

I nodded.

"Sounds good," he said.

"We'll go outside," Dillon said. "Let you ladies have your girl-time. Finn," he bowed. "Pleasure."

"Can you spare one?"

"Sure." Dillon handed her a cigarette from his pack.

"We'll be right outside," Tyler said, and he followed Dillon out the door.

Finn got some matches out of a drawer in the kitchen. "I'll give you the fast-forward version." She lit the cigarette. "We met on the boardwalk. He was playing his guitar. I sat and listened to a few songs because I didn't have anything to do, and I thought he was good, really good. I bought him lunch. We partied a little that night. He moved in a week later.

"It was cool. He was cool, but then things started getting weird. One night I got a phone call from him, and he was talking so fast I could hardly understand him. He said the cops were after him. I asked him where he was. He didn't know. All he could tell me was that he had borrowed someone's phone."

She smoked the cigarette hard and fast.

"I'd hear him pacing and talking to himself, instead of sleeping at night. He said our phone was tapped. He wouldn't talk to me in the apartment in anything over a whisper because of the wires. I was worried about him. He wouldn't let me call your folks."

"So you sent the e-mail."

"I sent the e-mail."

"In the e-mail you said he was, and I quote, 'into some serious shit.' What did you mean? The drugs?"

"He was using too much. I kept telling him. And the selling. I didn't think it was a good idea, but he'd met some guy who'd gotten him into it, before we were even together. He said the cops had found out and were watching our apartment."

I was having a hard time believing that Micah was caught up

in dealing and police, even though the guys at the surf shop had said something similar. Was he really that stupid? That far gone? "Did you believe him?"

"I don't know. It's possible. He had all kinds of people in and out of here—businessmen, surfers, moms, teenagers. Maybe the cops wanted to watch him so they could catch the bigger fish."

"Dillon said you were his sugar momma."

Finn laughed. "No."

"So he left because he thought the police were after him?"

"I don't know. He didn't exactly leave a note."

"Any idea of where he might have gone?"

"He could be anywhere. Some friends spotted him in Ocean Beach. Hell, he could still be in San Diego. He mentioned LA from time to time—that's where he wanted to go and do his music."

My stomach sank. LA was huge. If Micah had gone to LA, he was lost. He would be lost forever.

Finn pressed her cigarette into a turtle-shaped ashtray. She got up and went into the bathroom. I guessed she was finished with her story. I wanted her to keep talking, to tell me more about her time with Micah. She might be the last living connection I had to my brother.

"Where are you from?" I asked Finn when she emerged from the bathroom. I wanted to know more about her, about why Micah chose her.

"Ohio."

"How'd you get here?"

"A bus." She opened a jar of nail polish and started painting her nails a deep green.

"Did you always want to be an artist?"

"I used to carry a sketch pad with me when I was a kid." She didn't look up from her nails.

"I wanted to be a dancer," I said, trying to relate. "I used to close the door to my room and practice."

"What happened?"

"I wasn't very good or maybe I just lacked the confidence."

"Which one was it?"

I answered truthfully, "No confidence."

I sat and watched her for a while. I didn't know what else to say, and she clearly was over our conversation.

"Well," I finally said. "Thank you for . . . your time." I stood up to go.

"Rachel," she said.

I looked at her and there were tears in her eyes.

"I'm sorry I'm such a bitch. Your brother . . . God, what an asshole. You'd think he would have at least said good-bye. I mean, how much easier is it to say good-bye than I love you?" She waved her hands around to dry them. "Just don't give up, okay? He's fucked up, yes, but he was also—I mean, he *is* also hurting, you know?"

I looked away. I didn't want to hear about how much he was hurting. He chose to hurt. My parents, who couldn't sleep and watched TV instead of talking and avoided friends and family, didn't have a choice. I didn't have a choice. We were the ones who were hurting.

"When you're like Micah, when you're that low, you don't know how to get back up. And even when you get to the place where you want to call someone or go home, there's this enormous load of shame."

She spoke as if she carried some of that shame. I wondered how much she was talking about herself instead of Micah.

"He always talked about how smart you were, how good you were at everything. He told me about how you were in the top classes, about how everyone looked up to you. He was proud of you. I think he wished he could be more like you."

I knew she was laying it on pretty thick, but I wanted to believe her. I wanted to know that part of the old Micah was still out there.

"I know you may not believe me, but Micah loved you. He felt the most guilty about leaving you."

"Well," I said. I could see the day changing through her windows. "The sun will be down soon."

"He even told me about your ex."

I glared at her. "Keith?"

"Yeah. Micah said that he'd cheated on you and tried to ruin your reputation. I guess he beat the guy up pretty badly. Micah told him he would kill him if he ever came near you again."

I couldn't stop the tears from forming. So that explained why

Keith had been absent for a week not long after our breakup (he told everyone he had the flu), and why he'd avoided me when he returned to school. It was Micah. He had still cared.

"I just thought you should know."

"Thank you," I said, and smiled.

"It's so hard," she said.

"What's that?"

"When you love someone. It's hard to let them go."

"Yeah," I said, and headed for the door.

Chapter Twenty

Micah was exactly eleven months and seven days older than me, which meant he was a full year ahead of me in school. This also meant that I had the privilege of always being compared to him because he went first.

The first day of class always began with a roll call. "Rachel Stevens?" The teacher would stop and look up.

I'd raise my hand. "Present."

"I didn't know Micah had a sister." Pause.

"Yes."

This was followed by one of either two moves. The first was a raised eyebrow and tightly pursed lips. That was the signal for trouble. The other response was a large smile followed by, "Welcome."

Through seven years of elementary, two years of junior high, and three years of high school, I was known as Micah's younger sister. I often wondered if I had been the older, would he have been known as Rachel's younger brother. I doubted it.

We both played our roles with seeming ease. I was the A student. I took college prep and advanced classes. I served on student council. I ran and played volleyball. Micah, on the other hand, was an average student. He did not play sports or volunteer. He led a band, embraced his inner rebel in ninth grade, and didn't look back. He didn't cause trouble, he just didn't engage. He always stood a little apart, approaching life in a nonchalant kind of way. That is, until he met meth. He committed to her with a passion that I had never seen in him before.

When Micah came home from rehab, our quiet house became silent. It was as if we were holding our breath, waiting to see what Micah would do.

According to some book my parents had read, over 50 percent of users relapsed. For meth users, the statistics were worse. As if to account for this, drug programs believed relapse was actually part of recovery.

The first dinner after Micah had come home, my mom spoke quickly as if any space in the conversation frightened her. She talked about the weather, mild for that time of year. Then she spoke of her work, but saw that she was quickly losing us. She asked me about school. I said it was okay. She looked at me with wide eyes, pleading for my help. I looked down at the bloody steak I was eating. She asked my dad about his day. She did not talk about Micah's rehab or his drug situation, but it didn't matter. In my mind, everything she said circled back to Micah. She might as well have been saying, "Blah, blah, meth, blah, Micah, blah, rehab, drugs, blah, screwed up his life."

"This was good, Mom," Micah said after he finished dinner. "Much better than the food in rehab. Thanks."

He said the word and I could feel the house give a little, releasing some pressure, like an overfilled balloon.

"You're welcome," she said, and she gave my dad one of their "secret" knowing looks.

Micah stood up and took his plate and cup to the sink. He rinsed the plate, because there was nothing to scrape off, and put it in the dishwasher. Standing at the counter, he finished his water and added the glass to the rest of the dirty dishes.

"I think I'm gonna go chill for a while."

Out of the corner of my eye, I saw my mom tense.

"Chill?" my dad asked, an edge in his voice.

Micah stopped on his way to the stairs. He remained calm. If he was angry, he didn't show it. I felt as if I might lose it. "Yeah, I'm tired. I'll see you guys tomorrow." He grabbed the railing. "Maybe later we can talk about that job you were telling me about?"

My dad said, "Sure. Later."

"Good night, honey." My mom's nervous voice trailed after him.

I finished my food and repeated Micah's routine at the sink. I scraped chunks of gray and pink flesh into the garbage disposal and felt sick. My mom joined me at the sink, but my dad still sat at the table. I plopped myself down on our dark leather couch in the family room and quietly turned on the TV, so as not to irritate my dad.

I watched some show about a family, the kind with the distracting built-in laugh track. I observed the episode like a science experiment. It contained all of the usual suspects. Wild teenage daughter. Check. Loving but ignorant father. Check. Working mother, juggling it all. Check. Annoying little brother. Check.

The major conflict in the episode was that the daughter wanted to go to a party. Her parents said no. She went anyway. Under pressure, the little brother squealed. By the end of the half-hour show everything was resolved. The daughter, though upset at being grounded, understood that her parents were really trying to protect her because they loved her.

The last scene showed the whole family in the kitchen, standing over a cherry pie the mother had baked. There was no tension, nothing that needed further discussion, no lingering pain or hurt. I turned off the TV, feeling gypped at having wasted half an hour of my life.

Before I went to sleep that night, I washed my face, brushed my teeth, and read until I was good and tired. I said Micah's steps. But instead of turning on my fan, I lay back in the bed and listened for Micah. I tried picturing my brother through the thin wall that separated our rooms. I barely breathed.

The sounds of TV drifted up from downstairs. I could not hear anything coming from Micah's room. No pacing. No banging. Only quiet.

I reached over and turned the fan on medium. I stared at the ceiling while the fan purred, and thought, *We're going to be okay; we're going to be okay.* Then I drifted off to sleep.

Chapter Twenty-One

The fire crackled through faint rhythms from portable stereos and guitars and voices. It flickered, changing colors from sunset orange to sunrise yellow. The smells of sweet sage, ash, and beer blended into a familiar party scent. I wasn't close enough to the fire pit to enjoy the warmth, but at least I had on my sweatshirt. I covered my head with the hood. Since the sun had gone down, the temperature had dropped quite a bit. I felt sorry for Tyler; he must have been freezing in his T-shirt and jeans, but of course he tried not to show it.

After leaving Finn's apartment, Dillon said we needed to unwind. All the tension was starting to get him down. We grabbed a couple of burgers and asked around some more about Micah. After the sun disappeared, Dillon took us to a party on the beach, which had a hundred or so stoneys and surfers scattered around three fire pits.

In theory it sounded fun, but now that I was here, I wanted to leave. I didn't know anyone and felt that familiar shyness I got when I was at a party. In addition to being the usual designated driver, I was a typical wallflower. I never knew what to say. This party was no different.

I could hardly even see the people around me. Their faces were only partially illuminated by the light from the half-moon, stars, and fires, but I couldn't help but search the distorted faces for Micah. Even though Finn had proved to be a dead end and we were no closer to finding him, I felt hopeful. He was still out there. Finn had given me back a small piece of my brother. Maybe if I just stayed put, he'd come and brush up against me. Maybe I needed to stop searching.

Tyler wrapped his arms around his chest.

"You wanna move closer to the fire?" I asked him.

"Sure, if you want to."

We walked toward the nearest pit. A tall, leggy girl smiled at Tyler and started talking to him. The fire cast shadows across her face, and I could tell she was wasted. Tyler seemed at ease talking to the girl, but he kept glancing in my direction. Irritated, I walked away.

People huddled together, talking and smoking cloves, pot, and cigarettes. As I peered at their faces, most people nodded in my direction as if they knew me. A group of girls in bikini tops and shorts danced and laughed. Some coupled up and made out, not caring who watched.

I saw Dillon huddled around another fire pit with some guys. They drank out of red plastic cups. Dillon looked like he was in the middle of telling them a funny story. He wasn't a bad guy, I decided. My hands were cold away from the fire, so I shoved them into my pockets, where my fingers touched a small piece of paper. I pulled it out and saw that it was the number from Micah's pants. My body tensed. *It couldn't be that easy.*

Tyler made his way to me in the dark.

"Where's your friend?" I asked coyly.

"What friend?" he responded just as coyly.

"Dillon's over there." I pointed and put the number back inside my pocket. *No, it couldn't be that easy.*

We watched as everyone around Dillon started cracking up. "Entertaining as usual."

Dillon saw us and waved us over. He introduced us to his group.

"Tyler's a musician," he said to a guy named John who sat in the sand and picked at a guitar.

"Yeah, what instrument?" John asked.

"Bass, mainly."

"And guitar and he sings, too," Dillon said.

John held out his guitar to Tyler.

"No, man. I'm good."

"Come on," Dillon said. "Play something."

Tyler grinned in my direction and took the guitar from John. He started strumming a song that Micah had written two years ago. It was called "Stalker Girl," after this girl who used to follow him around from show to show. Sarcastic, with a cool hook, it kind of became their signature song. I had heard it many times, but always with Micah's voice and with a full band. Tyler never sang lead. He harmonized here and there, but you couldn't really hear him that well.

Tyler sang the opening line, "She's standing in the corner, red lips pouted in my direction," and I was shocked. He could sing, maybe even better than Micah.

Someone offered me a smoke and I passed. Already dizzy with pot fumes, I didn't need to be taking in any more.

Acoustic, the song had a totally different feel from the way I remembered. Tyler didn't seem at all shy about singing, either. Who knew? When he finished, everyone applauded.

"Keep going," John said.

Tyler glanced at me and I nodded. It's not like we had anywhere else to go.

Tyler launched into the Beatles' "Love Me Do." Then something funny happened. There was this kumbaya kind of moment where everything clicked. It was like when you're driving and a song comes on the radio and changes everything. You're transported somewhere else, even though you're just sitting in traffic or driving to school.

By the time Tyler began the second chorus, we were all singing with him. I couldn't say it was the most amazing sound, but it was pretty awesome. People started gathering around us. Another guitar appeared and requests were shouted out from the audience. After a couple more songs, Tyler handed the guitar back to John and we untangled ourselves from the crowd.

"I didn't know you could sing like that," I said as I plopped down on the sand a little closer to the water. I lay back to take in the night sky. Next to me, Tyler did the same.

The sky was huge and seemed extra full of stars. "Why didn't you ever take the lead in the band?"

"Micah's more of a front man. I don't mind being a supporting player."

Which meant Micah probably did, I thought.

"They're beautiful," I said, watching the stars. The sand felt cold beneath me, but it was so peaceful lying there with the sound of the ocean, I didn't want to move.

"I guess. You know, they're only giant balls of gas burning billions of miles away."

"You did not just do that," I said, but I couldn't help grinning.

"Maybe."

"Quote *The Lion King*."

"Pumbaa is one wise warthog."

I laughed and sat up. "Do you think he's still here? Be honest."

"If I were Micah, I'm wondering, what would keep me here?"

As Tyler spoke, a small black shape came toward us. It emerged slowly from the water, gradually getting bigger as it approached. As it got closer, I realized it was someone carrying a surfboard. A few seconds later, the large surfboard stuck itself in the sand next to me.

"Hello," a guy said, and shook his wet hair, getting some of it on my legs. "Sorry about that." He pulled a towel out of a bag that lay in the sand close to where we sat.

"No problem," I said.

"Here." He took his towel and wiped off one of my legs.

"I'm all right, thanks." He was a bit too forward for my liking.

"Awesome night." The surfer toweled off and faced the dark water.

Tyler had sat up and moved closer to me.

"You were surfing in the dark?" I asked, pointing to the black sea. I sometimes stated the obvious. I liked to think of it as processing out loud.

"Yeah. Not much in terms of waves, but I like to just sit there. Think. Commune with nature. Whatever you want to call it. It's a bit freaky because you can't see shit, but it's kind of cool, too. You should try."

"Oh no," I said. "I want to be able to see whatever's going to eat me."

The guy laughed.

"Nothing's going to eat you," Tyler said.

"There are sharks and jellyfish and who knows what else swimming near the surface in the middle of the night. I've seen the movies." Actually, I watched Shark Week every year. It was one of Micah's and my favorites; well, it used to be. We hadn't watched it this year. "My brother loved sharks. He wanted to go cage diving with the great whites before he died."

"South Africa, then. That'd be the place to do it."

"You been before?" Tyler asked.

The guy shook his head. "Name's Eric, by the way."

"Tyler, and this is Rachel." We all shook hands as if we were at some business meeting. "You live around here?"

Eric nodded. "A couple miles in. You?"

"No. Visiting."

I was about to ask him about Micah, when Eric unzipped his wetsuit and peeled it off his muscular body. He wrapped a towel around his midsection to change and I looked away.

"All right." Eric pulled his shirt over his head and stuffed his wet towel in his bag. "Enjoy." He picked up his board and started walking up the beach.

"Nice guy," I said. Tyler remained quiet.

"Not too bright."

I detected a tone. "Seemed fine to me."

"Surfing at night without a buddy? Stupid."

I wanted to argue, but I didn't. It had been a while since someone had been jealous over me.

Dillon stumbled up on us from behind, and I mean stumbled. He fell on top of Tyler and kind of flipped over in the sand.

"Been looking for you guys all over. Thought you might have bailed."

"You found us," I said, not thrilled.

He crawled over to where I sat. "I got two more leads." He put his arm around me, and I had to pry it off. I hated being around people when they were drunk.

We helped Dillon to his feet. He was kind of, well, as he would have said, shit-faced.

"I got it." Dillon pushed us away and steadied himself. He closed his eyes and stood with his arms out at both sides, like a guy balancing on a wire. "Ready," he said, and opened his eyes.

We walked back up the beach to Dillon's car.

"Keys." Tyler held out his hand to Dillon in the parking lot.

Dillon looked as if he might challenge, but he just unchained them from the loop on his shorts and tossed them to Tyler. It took a bit of maneuvering, but we ended up leaving the lot like this: the three of us crammed together in the front with Tyler driving and me in the middle. My bare legs touched both Dillon's and Tyler's, so I scooted more toward Tyler.

Dillon directed us away from Mission Beach and inland. We drove down a narrow suburban street with eerie yellow streetlights. Shadows grew and became more prevalent in the low light, suggesting danger. I imagined eyes following Dillon's car as it slowly made its way down the street. Total darkness or total light would have been better.

We stopped in front of a plain, one-story, stuccoed white house. It was almost invisible because it looked like so many others. A hedge of small shrubs separated the perfectly manicured yard from the neighbors. Behind drawn blinds, light shone from a couple of rooms. Someone was home.

"So . . . you think Micah's here?" I asked.

"Maybe."

Dillon leaned back on the seat and closed his eyes. "When you get to the door, just ask if they have any shit."

"Shit?" I asked.

"Yeah."

I was confused.

"It's what people call meth when they go looking for it," Tyler said.

That hadn't been on the list of names my research had turned up. "Why?"

"Because it tastes like shit," Dillon said, slurring his words. "Are you going to go or what?"

"Maybe you should stay in the car," Tyler said to me.

"No," I looked at Dillon, whose eyes were closed like he was already asleep. "I'm going."

"Just stick close to me, please," Tyler whispered before we left the car.

I followed Tyler up the small brick pathway to the front door. Tyler knocked three times and the door opened. A young woman with short blond hair, wearing a pink sweat suit, stood in the doorway and looked us up and down.

"Yes?"

"We heard you might have some shit," Tyler said.

She opened the door and motioned for us to come inside. I hesitated for a moment, getting this feeling that if I crossed that threshold, there would be no turning back. Micah's face flashed in my mind, giving me courage. I held my breath and entered.

Inside the house, everything looked like you'd expect it to from the outside: a living room with a couch and a love seat, a TV mounted on the wall, a hallway with doors to what were probably bedrooms. The TV played one of my favorite shows, and some people sat on a couch watching. One guy, a surfer type, turned his head and nodded "hey" when he saw us standing there. No Micah.

I was about to show the woman his picture, when she asked, "How much?"

"Just a hit," Tyler said, holding out some cash.

What was he doing? I pretended that buying drugs was a normal part of my life and that I did it all the time. Which meant that I looked away, shoved my hands in my pockets, and acted disinterested.

The girl took the money and went into the kitchen. "Cute" was written on the butt of her sweatpants. While she was gone, one of the doors opened down the hallway and a man in a tie and gray slacks walked past us. I recognized the smell on him—kind of like a shower curtain. He smelled like Micah did when he used.

"Here," the girl said when she returned. She held out a small clear bag with some crystals. "You can use the room with the open door if you'd like."

"Thanks," Tyler said, taking the bag and my hand. She went to sit with the others on the couch.

Tyler flipped on the light switch and closed the door behind us. A single bed lay against the wall next to a desk with a lamp. There was also a small chair with a basket of children's books next to it. A basketball hoop, the kind that you played with a Nerf ball, was attached to the back of the door. Micah had had one when he was younger.

I sat on the bed and wondered, *Had Micah ever sat here?* It's not like he would have left me a sign like *Micah was here*, scratched into the wall, though I looked for any clues. My hands felt the blue comforter. Maybe he'd smoked and sat in the chair reading *Curious George*, a childhood favorite.

Drug paraphernalia, a pipe and a lighter, rested on the desk. A one-stop drug house. Convenient. Tyler set the bag of crystals down next to the pipe.

I got up and stood next to him. The bag was so small. So insignificant.

"Doesn't seem like much," I said.

"It's enough."

I picked up the bag and cradled it in my hand. Crazy to think how the mess with Micah started with this. Opening the bag, I dumped its contents into my palm. It hardly weighed anything at all. I bent to smell it. Nothing. Odorless. My body suddenly shook like it was cold, except it wasn't. A strong desire came over me; I wanted to try it. I wanted to see what Micah saw, to feel what he felt. To know what it was that stole him from me, as if then I might understand it better. All I needed was a small glimpse of his world. I could taste the crystals, just a little prick of the tongue. No one would know, except Tyler. Who would he tell? It probably wouldn't even make me high.

As if he'd heard my thoughts, Tyler reached for my hand that held the bag and closed his around mine. He walked me over to the small bathroom attached to the bedroom. He turned on the hot water in the sink, but then he pulled away. He gave me the choice. I stood there for a while. In the end, I watched the crystals disappear down the drain. The water burned my hand, but I kept it there, even though it turned bright red.

We walked back down the hallway. The woman in the pink sweats got up from the couch.

"Thanks," Tyler said.

She led us to the front door.

"I wanted to know if you've seen him," I said, and showed her my worn picture of Micah.

"No." She didn't even look at it. "You can try them." She pointed to the couch.

At least they looked at the photo, but no one knew Micah. The chances, of course, had been miniscule all along. We were at some random drug house. One out of probably thousands in the city. Was I prepared to go to each one?

"You a girlfriend?" the woman asked me when I was back outside. She leaned against the frame of the door.

"No, sister."

"Want some advice?"

Not really, I thought. I shrugged.

"Stop looking." She flicked her cigarette down on the walkway. "When he's ready, he'll come to you." Then she shut the door.

As we walked to Dillon's car, I rubbed the palm of my hand, which pulsed red and raw in the cool night air.

Chapter Twenty-Two

In the car, Dillon was passed out in the front seat with his mouth open. Tyler tried waking him by saying his name and then shaking him, but he wouldn't budge. I slapped him in the face. He only grunted.

Tyler got behind the wheel again, and I sat on the other side of Dillon. We pulled away just as another car drove up to the house. I didn't even bother to see if it was Micah because I knew it wouldn't be.

The first corner Tyler took sent Dillon sliding toward me. His head fell on top of my shoulder. I pushed him toward Tyler.

"I'm driving."

"I know, but I don't want him on me. His breath stinks."

We alternated shoving Dillon back and forth between us a couple of times before Tyler stopped at a curb.

"Here, help me move him to the backseat," Tyler said.

He grabbed Dillon's upper body, and I pushed the rest of him toward Tyler. As Tyler pulled him out of the car, I ran around and grabbed his legs again. I stumbled under the weight of him. For a short guy, Dillon must have been all muscle. Tyler lost his grip, and he and Dillon fell onto the asphalt. Tyler and I froze, waiting for Dillon to shout or something, but Dillon's eyes stayed closed. I giggled.

"Come on," Tyler said, but he laughed too. He picked himself up, got hold of Dillon again, and backed him into the backseat. I struggled to help Tyler. Eventually, Dillon lay facedown on the black leather seat with his butt up in the air.

I groaned. "We can't leave him like that."

Tyler pushed Dillon into a sitting position, and I latched a seat belt around him.

"Do you know where we are?" I asked Tyler when we got back into the front seat.

"I have an idea, but my phone would be good right about now."

"Let's just drive." I leaned the side of my head against the window. "I don't care where."

Tyler started the car again.

"We could even drive straight to morning," I said. It had to be past midnight already.

"All right, straight to morning."

The day had been a total wash. No phone. No Micah. Car stolen. God, I kept forgetting about that one. No way home.

Tyler turned on the radio and tapped the steering wheel with his fingers. He sang along to Katy Perry's "Teenage Dream." He sounded ridiculous, but that was the point. He made me laugh, and I started to think the day hadn't been a total wash.

Tyler said he couldn't just drive without any direction, so he decided to alternate between turning right and left at each intersection he came to. We zigzagged our way past homes and stores and gas stations. Nothing looked familiar and yet everything looked familiar.

I glanced back at Dillon. He snored pretty loudly.

"I would hate to sleep in the same bed with him." I cringed thinking how that must have sounded. I hadn't meant for it to come out that way. "I mean, you know—"

Tyler didn't even notice. "I know, think about his poor mom. You could hear that through the walls."

"You getting tired?" I asked him.

"I could use a Coke."

"I think I saw a convenience store a couple blocks back. Remember?"

"Yeah."

Tyler turned the car around and found the market. He parked in the lot and asked if I wanted anything. I asked for something to drink and insisted that I pay this time. Tyler didn't argue as he took the cash from me.

I waited in the car with Dillon. There was a pay phone out

front. Remembering the number in my pocket, I pulled it out. *Now or never,* I thought. I found some change in Dillon's car.

Before I could chicken out, I dialed the number. It rang five times before I heard the click of someone answering.

"Hello," said a male voice.

"Hello?" I said, but no one responded. I heard breathing on the other end. "Hello? Can you hear me?" It sounded like someone was riding in a car. "Micah?" I whispered.

The phone clicked. The person had hung up.

My heart tightened. I dialed the number again. Maybe whoever was on the other end couldn't hear me. My calls always got dropped in a certain section of town. It rang a couple of times again before heading to voice mail. "The person you are trying to reach is not available now." *Click.* I didn't even get to leave a message.

Tyler exited the store just as I hung up the phone.

"Calling someone?" He looked at me, puzzled.

I shrugged. "Just testing it out. Never used one before."

"A pay phone? Huh. Neither have I."

I shoved the piece of paper back into my pocket.

He handed me my drink. "You okay?" he asked.

"Of course," I said, but avoided his eyes.

"I got directions back to Dillon's."

"Wow. A guy who asks for directions."

Tyler ignored me. "We're about twenty minutes away. We could crash there for the night."

"Whatever." I thought about the voice and the breathing on the other end of the line. It probably wasn't Micah anyway. It wasn't like he had a signature breath.

My chest hurt. I held my hand over it, as if saying the pledge of allegiance, as if I could hold my heart together, or that applying some pressure would stop it from aching. It worked for nosebleeds, not heart trouble.

When I was younger, I was diagnosed with a heart murmur. It meant that I had an extra whooshing sound between beats. The doctor said it was harmless and nothing to worry about. The only time it seemed to matter was when I went to the dentist or filled out paperwork for sports.

But Micah had been pretty upset about it. He'd thought it meant that my heart might stop. There was a time when he wanted to make sure it was working right, especially after we had been running around in the backyard. He called it a "heart check." He would lean his head against my chest, close his eyes, and count. When he'd listened to ten beats, he'd lift his head and tell me that I sounded good, so we could still play. He said he could hear the murmur, but I knew that was impossible without a stethoscope. Micah insisted, though, saying that he heard my heart whisper.

"You sure you're good?" Tyler asked, pulling into the street.

"Yeah." I held my breath and released it slowly. Maybe I was having a heart attack. My pulse was racing. No, I was too young. I thought I could hear the whooshing sound of the murmur, as my pulse pounded in my ears. Maybe this was a panic attack. I counted to ten.

"Tell me if you want me to pull—"

"Watch out!" A small cat ran into the road in front of the car.

Tyler swerved and hit the curb, as well as a trash can, before slamming on the brakes.

"Shit," he said.

"Where's the cat?" I scrambled out of the car.

"A cat?"

"Or a kitten or something." I looked up and down the street and sidewalk. I held my heart again, anticipating fresh roadkill.

"Rach, you can't do that." Tyler assessed the damage to the car. No dents, only two small scratches where we'd hit the trash can. "You scared the hell out of me."

"Where is it?" I felt tears forming.

Tyler took off his hat and ran his hand through his hair. "What?"

"The cat." I got down on my hands and knees and looked underneath the car. It wasn't there. I stood back up and hugged my arms to my chest.

"We didn't kill it," Tyler said softly.

"Maybe." I sniffed. I couldn't see the cat anywhere. I eyed the scratches on the bumper. "He'll never notice."

"Hey," Dillon called from the backseat. He sipped on my drink, which I had left in the car.

"Look who's back from the dead," Tyler said.

Dillon grinned. "Where are we?" He stretched and yawned really big.

"Nowhere, man. Just heading back to your place."

Tyler and I returned to the car. Dillon leaned forward and placed his arms on the back of the front seat.

"Still no Micah, I take it."

"Nope."

Dillon sat back and pulled out his phone. I watched the street through the passenger window. Tyler kept glancing at me, but I pretended not to notice.

"All right. We're set."

"What?" Tyler asked.

"One a.m. A department store's parking lot."

I looked at Tyler and he nodded as if to say, one more time.

"Not making any promises."

Promises. I turned from Tyler and faced the front. Promises were made to be broken. I pulled the piece of paper out of my pocket. The voice on the other line hadn't been Micah's. I had been foolish to think it could have been that easy. And even if it had . . . He had hung up on me. Why did I even bother?

Rolling down the window, I stuck my hand outside and released the number. It flew away. My free hand floated up and down, riding the wind, before I pulled it back inside.

Chapter Twenty-Three

"You told me you wouldn't," I said.

Micah sat on his bed and strummed his guitar. It wasn't plugged in, so the notes were thin and tinny.

"Your words. They're supposed to mean something."

"It's not a big deal." He started humming and closed his eyes.

"You have a problem." Understatement of the year.

"Rach! Quit riding me. Go study, or whatever you do."

I didn't budge from the frame of his bedroom door. He continued to play.

"Look," he said, probably knowing I was being stubborn and could stand there all night, "I partied too hard. I know. But I've got it handled. The worry act is unnecessary."

"But—"

He rolled his eyes and put on his headphones. I hesitated. If he lied to me once, how many times had he lied before? I knew the answer—every time. For some reason I had refused to see it before; maybe I didn't want to see it. I needed to tell Mom and Dad. But how could I, without his seeing it as a huge betrayal? He would hate me.

I turned to leave.

"Hey, listen to this new one I'm working on. What do you think?"

Micah took off his headphones and began singing. I reentered his room and sat on his bed next to him, like I always did when he played me a new song. His voice asked me to forget about the night before, to trust him, as he sang something about being pissed about a girl who'd left him for another guy. He sounded so normal, so good.

"Well?" he asked when he stopped playing. "It's not done, but what do you think so far?"

"Funny," I said.

"Yeah, I was going for kind of a humoristic take on the whole being-dumped thing."

My phone buzzed. It was a text from Keith.

"It's good. Gotta go."

"Say hi to Keith for me," Micah said, all high-voiced.

"Shut up," I said, and got up from the bed.

"We're cool, right?" he asked when I reached the door.

"Yeah," I said, because the truth was becoming much more painful. "We're cool."

"Promise?" Micah smiled and put his headphones back on before I could answer.

"Promise," I said softly.

Chapter Twenty-Four

We cruised into an empty lot and parked behind a group of bushes as far away from the store's entrance as possible. Supposedly, a dealer who knew Micah liked to do business here in the early hours of the morning. A sense of desperation came over me, probably because it was our last-ditch effort to find Micah.

Tyler shut off the engine. We rolled down the front windows so it wouldn't get all foggy inside.

The huge warehouse seemed to stare down at me. I hated this particular store. Everything felt loud and cheap when you entered. The lighting instantly gave me a headache. Every tag said *Made in China* or wherever. Kids always cried and ran down the aisles. I wished someone would ban or annihilate the business.

"So now what?" I asked, kind of in a grumpy mood.

"We wait," Dillon said.

"It's already a little after one. Maybe you should text him to make sure."

"Already on it. Now we sit tight."

"Rach," Tyler said, as if he were warning me to back off.

"All right. We wait."

I hadn't had much experience waiting for dealers, so I didn't know if they were punctual or not. Dillon and Tyler didn't seem to think they were. In my opinion, it didn't make the best business sense to keep your customers waiting.

Sitting in the dark made me nervous. By 1:25 I was edgy.

"Say something," I said to Tyler.

"Like what?"

"Anything."

"I wonder how many cars it'd take to fill this lot."

I looked at him with my *Seriously?* expression.

"Four hundred," Dillon said from the back.

"I was thinking more."

"Maybe."

"Your turn," Tyler said to me.

"What do you mean, my turn?"

"Say something."

I didn't know what to say.

"Not so easy, huh?" Tyler said.

I looked out the window at the empty parking lot. The guy wasn't going to show.

"So, you having a good summer so far?" Tyler asked me.

I laughed at Tyler's attempt at small talk. "Yeah, you?" I put both feet on the dashboard.

"Pretty good. Work. Sleeping in."

"You still work at the music store?" I asked.

"Yep."

"You get a discount?" Dillon asked.

"Twenty percent."

"That's decent."

The car became silent again. I knew I would have to ask a question to keep the conversation going, but I didn't want to have to carry it.

"My first job was at a gas station," Dillon offered. "I didn't get free gas, though."

"I babysit. Not tons of money, but it's easy," I added.

Silence again. Tyler and I hadn't had any awkward conversations all day. Dillon must've changed the equation.

"This might be him," Dillon said as a small dark car entered the parking lot. It parked on the opposite side of the lot. Not close, but not that far away. Thankfully, the bushes hid us.

"What do we do?" I whispered.

"I'll go talk to him. Give me that picture you've been showing around." Dillon held out his hand for the photo.

Dillon was about to open the car door, when another dark car entered the lot and slowly drove up to the first car. It parked right next to the black car, and three guys got out.

"Get down," Dillon said.

I sank into the seat. I wanted to ask what was wrong, but this time I sensed it was best to keep my mouth shut. We couldn't see anything, but with the windows rolled down we could make out male voices. At first they sounded normal, pleasant, like a group of guys talking. I couldn't understand what they were saying exactly. And then I heard the first hit.

"Shit," Dillon whispered. I saw him trying to peek out the back window.

I heard another hit. It wasn't like the sound effects in the movies. Flesh on flesh didn't sound like slaps. It was like listening to my mom tenderize a slab of meat before cooking it. I wondered if that's how it had sounded when Micah beat up Keith. How many times had he hit Keith? Had Keith gotten a few punches in?

I had never been in a fight; well, only the verbal kind. In the seventh grade, this girl Marisol said something ugly about Micah on the bus. I told her to take it back, but she wouldn't. So I called her a bitch under my breath. Unfortunately, she heard me, and in the heat of the moment, I'd forgotten that she got off at the same stop as Micah and me.

As soon as the bus pulled away, she pushed me from behind.

I wasn't prepared for it, so I went sprawling onto the sidewalk. My knee still has a faint scar from where I scraped it across the pavement. By the time I stood up, Marisol dropped her bag on the ground and was ready to pounce on me. But before she could, Micah grabbed her from behind and pinned her arms to the side. That gave me enough time to run, which I did, all the way home.

I opened the door and was about to shut it when I saw Micah wasn't far behind me. After giving me a head start, he had dropped Marisol and taken off. Marisol was big for her age, so Micah had probably been scared of her too. We laughed about it over a bag of chips, but I think I would have passed out if she had actually punched me.

How many hits could someone take before passing out? I wondered. The sound of punches and grunts and heavy breathing kept coming in a steady staccato. There were kicks now, thudding between the hits. I wanted Tyler to roll up the window. I held my hands over my ears and looked at Tyler. He was frightened, which made me even more scared.

"We should get out of here," Tyler whispered.

"What if they follow?" Dillon asked.

"They could see us now," Tyler said. "You want to take that chance?"

"No. We're okay. We're too hidden."

"Dillon—"

"They could see my plates and then what? I'm dead."

Dillon had a point. Tyler and I would be in the clear, but they could track him and show up at his house.

The beating finally stopped. But that was followed by the opening of a door, more voices. The slam of a trunk. Footsteps.

I slowed my breathing, but my pulse raced. I strained to hear. Were the steps coming closer? Maybe. My hand gripped the door handle, ready to fling it open, so I could run if I had to. An ignition started. A car peeled out of the lot. None of us said anything. We remained still, listening. My breathing was shallow. I could hear Tyler's. Dillon crept up to peer out the window. He opened the door.

Wait, I said in my mind, terrified at what might happen.

He stepped outside, crouching low to the ground. Tyler and I sat up a little to watch him. Dillon crawled away from the car, and then stood up behind the bushes and looked around. My heart pulsed in an irregular, rapid rhythm.

"We're good," he said.

Tyler and I both got out of the car and joined Dillon. The first car was still in the lot. A dark mound lay on the ground next to it. Dillon started walking toward the car. I didn't want to follow, but Tyler held out his hand for mine. I grabbed it and he pulled me toward him protectively.

I walked, looking all around me, afraid someone would jump out of hiding. But there was only Tyler, Dillon, me, and the crumpled body of a young man I could now make out on the ground.

"Hey," Dillon said as he approached the body.

No sound. But there was that rusty, sweet smell again. Blood.

Dillon reached out with his foot and gently nudged the man. The body didn't move. Dillon bent over the body and motioned Tyler to him. Tyler let go of my hand and helped Dillon roll the man onto his back.

I gasped. Blood covered his face, what was left of it, and pooled on the ground. Swelling had already sealed shut both of his eyes. His nose was squashed and cut up. His mouth curved into a jagged scar. Gashes covered his hands from where he'd probably tried to protect himself. Tyler reached out and held the man's wrist.

"He's alive."

As if to let us know for certain, the man moaned.

"Barely," Dillon said. "Help me push him onto his side."

As they did, I saw a wound bleeding on the back of his head. The man tried to say something, but I couldn't understand him. He coughed and blood spilled from his mouth.

I bent down and put my hand to his chest. "What's his name?"

"I don't know," said Dillon.

"It's going to be all right," I said to the man. "We'll help you." I took his bloodied hand in mine. "We've got to get him help."

Tyler and Dillon didn't say anything; they just stood looking down at the wounded man.

"What?" I asked.

"Check his pockets for a phone," Dillon said.

Trying not to hurt him, I gently looked and found one in his back pocket.

"Here."

Dillon dialed 911.

"Head wounds bleed a lot," I told them. I blocked Keith's face from my mind.

"All right. They're on their way." Dillon removed the Sim card and pocketed the phone. "Can't have them tracing my texts with this."

"We can't just leave him," I said.

"We have to," Tyler said.

I stood up and glared at both of them, even though I knew they were right. The police would ask us all kinds of questions, why we were here, what we saw, etc. . . . Who knew what kind of trouble we'd be in?

Dillon peeked inside the car. "They didn't even take all the weed. What a waste."

"Don't even think about it," Tyler said.

We jogged to our car.

"She can't get in like that." Dillon opened the trunk and took out a shirt. "Here, wipe off the blood." He grabbed a cigarette from the pack in his back pocket and lit it.

My hands were smeared with the man's blood. I tried to wipe them, but I was shaking. Tyler took the shirt and gently rubbed my hands clean. He threw the dirtied shirt into the trunk and maneuvered me into the front seat. This time Dillon drove and Tyler sat between us.

"Shit," Dillon said, when we were quite a distance away. He laughed nervously. "Well, kids, I think we'll call it a night." He took a long drag and blew the smoke out of the small opening in the window. "Shit."

I suddenly felt claustrophobic. Dillon stopped at a red light, and I saw a small park in the distance. I reached for the door.

"What are you doing?" Tyler asked.

"I've got to get out of here." I opened the door and climbed out; Tyler followed me. Since it was so late, we were the only ones stopped at the intersection. I turned back to Dillon. "Thank you."

"You sure? You guys could crash at my house." Dillon said the words, but I could tell he wanted to be cut free.

"I know."

"I'll let you know if I hear anything about Micah." The light turned green, and Dillon waved and drove off. I watched the car's taillights for a moment with my hands in the pockets of my hoodie.

Tyler followed me across the street to the park. The swings hung limply in front of us.

"You were pretty amazing back there," Tyler said. "That guy—most people wouldn't have touched him."

"No one deserves that, not even drug dealers."

I walked over and sat in one of the swings. Tyler came up behind me and began to push, just a little, just enough to glide me back and forth. I didn't help him by pumping my legs, but I picked them up so my feet wouldn't drag across the dirt. I shook as if I were cold, so I held the chain with both hands and tried to ignore the moaning of rusty hinges.

Tyler gave me a big push, and I leaned back so I could go as high as I could. He pushed me again and again, his hands a steady constant on the middle of my back. With each new height, I closed my eyes and pictured myself flying away, like I used to as a kid. I wished I could go back, be a kid again, when everything was simple and the bad guys existed only in movies. Where there were no ex-boyfriends, no drugs. Where Micah and I were innocent and pure.

Chapter Twenty-Five

After sitting on the swings for a while, we started walking, not saying anything to each other. Tyler seemed to know where he was going, so I followed him without question. I didn't look around the streets anymore. I didn't look into the eyes of any late-night stragglers we passed. I didn't do a double take every time I saw a guy with brown hair and tattoos. I had given up. We would not find him today; maybe we'd never find him.

At a bus stop, Tyler read the map showing the times and locations.

"Well, we can wait for the next one," he said.

"When's that?" I sat down on the bench, tired, more from the emotion of the day than the walking.

"Six thirty. Actually, that's probably in only a couple of hours."

I closed my eyes and rested my head against the tagged Plexiglas.

"We can take the bus to the train station, which will at least get us to Escondido. Someone could easily pick us up there."

I lay down on the bench. An image of a homeless person covering himself in a blanket appeared in my mind. "All we need is some newspaper."

"We are not sleeping out here. Your brother would kill me."

"Hmm. Good thing he isn't here, then."

"I'll figure something out. Don't worry."

"Oh, I'm sure you will," I said, and stretched out on my back and looked up at the sky. The stars had all but disappeared with all the light pollution in this part of the city.

Tyler smashed his hands into his front pockets. He looked up and down the street. He seemed very nervous. I probably should have tried to reassure him, tell him that everything was going to be all right, that I didn't blame him for not finding Micah. Instead, I traced the distant skyline with a finger. The buildings were industrial and square. Where the neighborhoods gathered together, the shapes became more distinct, though still similar. My finger veered up to a point and then dropped sharply.

"Come on," I said, sitting up, grabbing my backpack, and slinging it over my shoulder.

"Where?"

I pointed. "Someplace that can maybe help."

He studied my face for a few moments and then, resigned, said, "Lead the way."

I led us as well as I could, though it was the middle of the night in a city I didn't know. We crossed a busy intersection with a gas station and food mart. I turned onto a side road, where we walked past homes lit with porch lights.

In front of one home, water trickled from a small fall into a little pond. Small animal-shaped shrubs dotted the lawn. It seemed so peaceful, yet I had no idea what was going on inside. I stopped and held up my hand.

"You sure you know where you're going?" Tyler asked.

I retraced the tip of the building in the air. It guided me like a star in the night.

"Yes."

The neighborhood homes morphed into multistory apartment buildings, which cropped up between run-down shacks that passed themselves off as duplexes. Tyler walked closer to me. If the day had proven anything, he was awfully protective. But I didn't mind.

We passed under a broken streetlight. One block over, the neighborhood changed again, becoming a little nicer. It was strange how just one block could alter everything.

I stopped again, this time in front of a small white building with a tall steeple. No lights shone, inside or outside. I walked up to the large, solid wooden doors and touched them. They were simple, without carvings or markings. Two huge black rings acted as doorknobs. I tried pulling on one of them, but the door was locked.

"What are you doing?" Tyler whispered.

I sank to the ground and leaned my body against the cold wooden door. Across the street stood a twenty-four-hour liquor store. I smiled, imagining how both organizations must fight for people's souls as they confessed one night and sinned another. Both places probably did good business.

I didn't know what kind of a church it was or if it had a pastor or priest. It didn't matter what religion met there on Sundays. I knew that I had a better chance of talking to God inside that building than anywhere else.

Tyler knelt down next to me. "This is the place?" he asked softly.

"This is the place," I repeated.

His hand held one of the thick knockers. Over Tyler's shoulder, I watched an older man leave the liquor store with a large paper bag in his hands.

"It doesn't matter," I said.

Tyler stood up and held his free hand out to me. "Come on."

I didn't move.

"Come on! Let's find another way in." I grabbed his outstretched hand. It was cold, but it warmed my skin.

Large bushes grew alongside the church, so we practically had to hug the walls. There were a couple of tall, rounded windows on the side. Tyler tried a window. Locked. He tried another one. Also locked. We walked around to the other side of the church, and he pulled on the latch of another set. This time it gave. With a bit of a tug, he pulled open a window.

He climbed in first and pulled me up after him. I held on to Tyler with both hands and stumbled when he set me down.

"Sorry," I said, thankful that he couldn't see me blushing in the dark.

Almost instantly, a feeling of calm came over me. A group of unlit candles in tall glass jars stood together on a table next to me. I picked up a match, struck it, and lit all of them. The candlelight glowed to the corners of the room. Simple wooden pews lined both sides of a red-carpeted aisle in the small church. At the front, Jesus's dying body hung ominously from a large cross above a pulpit where the priest would speak. It was definitely a Catholic church. The Jesus on the cross was a giveaway. Protestant churches, like Michelle's, had Jesus too. He just wasn't usually on the cross. Tyler closed the window behind us.

"You think we'll get in trouble if someone finds us?" I whispered.

"You mean like, could they charge us with breaking and entering? That depends. We're not going to steal anything, right?"

"No."

"Maybe trespassing, then. But it's a church. They're supposed to help people in need. If someone comes, we'll just tell them that we didn't have anywhere else to go."

Tyler's reasoning helped me relax. In a way, he was right. We didn't have anywhere else to go. It was still hours before we could catch the bus.

On the wall underneath the candles was a picture of Jesus carrying a cross. "It's the second image of the Via Dolorosa," I said.

"What's that?" Tyler asked, as if he'd never seen it before.

"The Way of Sorrows."

"I didn't know you went to church."

"I only go on Easter. It's something my mom makes us do. Let's just say I've heard the same message a few times now and some of it stuck. It's like a picture book. See?" I pointed to the other paintings. "You can follow the story around the room." In the one Tyler stood in front of, Jesus already looked tired. I felt sorry for Him. He didn't know how far He'd still have to go.

"Why are we whispering?"

I shook my head. Tyler held his arms up in the air as if to say, "What?" Of course you whispered in a church. I didn't really know why, but everyone did, so it didn't matter why.

I moved across the aisle to the other side of the room, where other Stations of the Cross paintings hung above tables with the same tall glass jars. I lit a couple more candles. I couldn't remember the significance behind lighting candles, but at the moment, the significance was that we needed more light. I hoped what I was doing wasn't offensive. But I had heard somewhere that it was better to ask for forgiveness rather than permission. I figured I'd ask for forgiveness later, if need be.

Illuminated by candlelight, the church felt medieval, as if at any moment a monk could walk by.

Tyler stood at the pulpit. He spread his arms wide and looked up at the Jesus staring down at him.

I followed the Way of Sorrows for a bit. Jesus carried His cross. Jesus fell. Jesus faced His mother. He fell again. I stopped in front of Jesus being nailed to the cross. This Jesus was more familiar—skinny, almost emaciated, and naked except for a small white cloth tied around His waist. His chest stuck out awkwardly from the wooden beam. His stomach caved in on itself. His legs hung like frail bone.

But it was His face that contained the harshest truth. His eyes were sunk into their sockets and turned upward toward heaven. His cheekbones were drawn in severe lines, making His agony more pronounced. The truth was, I knew this face. I had seen that pain a few times that day. I had also seen it on my brother. Who would have thought? Jesus Christ had something in common with a meth addict.

I walked to the center of a pew and sat down on the hard bench. No cushions. Maybe the priest wanted the people to feel uncomfortable and be reminded of Christ's suffering.

We had once visited some old cathedrals in Montreal on a family vacation. I had felt a little funny walking in on such an intimate moment as people praying, but our tour guide said it was okay, if we were quiet. The people sat with their heads bowed, their hands in their laps. Some of them kneeled.

Under the bench in front of me, I saw the kneeling bar. I pulled it down and slid onto it. I brought my hands in front of me and folded them as I had seen others do.

I closed my eyes and waited. I heard Tyler walk quietly to a row of seats behind me, the keys on his belt loop jangling, then scraping the wood as he sat down. My breathing slowed. The back of my eyelids turned black and yellow, then black with orangey red spots. I tried to remain completely still and give in to the silence around me. It was so quiet. I thought I could hear the flame moving on the wicks of the candles. It sounded like a breath.

I tried to clear my mind, to think of nothing. But I couldn't just imagine nothing, so I pictured an empty space, wide open like a field of dry yellow grass. Then I envisioned the field that surrounded our home when I was little. In the late summer, when the winds picked up, giant tumbleweeds pulled themselves off the ground and chased Micah and me down our street. We'd run screaming and laughing into the house. He'd always beat me to the door, then hold it open, yelling for me to hurry up. I'd get there just in time and he'd shut the door right before they caught us. A couple seconds later, we'd hear the sound of the monster weeds slamming against the door. The next morning, the whole street would be covered with broken yellow sticks and twigs.

I cleared the street from my mind and focused instead on the field before the tumbleweeds. The lemony grass, like stalks of wheat, swayed along with a light breeze.

I learned how to meditate from my freshman English teacher, a small woman with short, wispy white hair and a nose ring. She always looked like she needed the exercise more than we did. She started off every class playing instrumental music from India or something as we walked in.

At first, we all fought her. She sounded crazy, closing her eyes, talking about picturing a safe place. Some of the guys would laugh and make fun of her. But eventually we got used to it, even the ones who resisted. I looked forward to it, and after the thing with Keith, it actually helped me through many of the tough days.

On days when we had a sub, at the start of class one of us would press play on the stereo system and begin the breathing exercise. It always freaked out the subs. They weren't used to seeing thirty-five fourteen-year-olds sitting quietly with their eyes closed, opening them all at once when the music ended.

In the dark of the church, I waited for something to come to me. I cleared the field from my thoughts and began again. Keith's face appeared, along with the words he'd written about me. This time I didn't try to push him aside.

"Keith was my first." I got off my knees and sat on the bench. "Great choice, huh?"

Tyler moved to sit next to me.

I put my feet up on the bench in front of me. Tyler did the same, as if we were sitting in a movie theater and staring at a big screen, instead of the big dying Jesus. "When I broke up with him and he wrote all those things, I thought I would die. The truth is that he was the one cheating. I never said anything."

"Maybe you should have."

"Yeah, maybe. It wouldn't have changed anything. I bet you're wondering why I stayed with him." I was embarrassed by the reason, but I kept going, in a way eager to let the truth out. "I liked the *idea* of Keith, if that makes sense. It sounds so cliché, but that's the thing about clichés, they have some truth in them, right? Really, I didn't want to be alone. So maybe I deserved it."

"You know that's not true," Tyler said.

The problem was, there was a small part of me that believed I had deserved it, that God was punishing me for not helping Micah when I could have.

Tyler was quiet for a few moments.

"So if it's confession time, I guess it's my turn, right?" Tyler sat up and turned to face me on the bench, sitting cross-legged.

I couldn't tell if he was teasing. "What do you mean?" I asked warily.

"You think you're the only one with secrets?" he whispered.

I smiled. "Probably not."

Tyler took a deep breath and then said very quickly, "I used to wet the bed. My mom had to buy me diapers until I was ten."

"No!" I was shocked.

"Totally true. I never went to sleepovers. The shrink said it had something to do with my father and him being an alcoholic."

My mouth hung open, but I closed it and asked, "You went to a shrink?"

"For three years. Okay, number two—no the shrink is two, secret number three: I didn't kiss a girl until I was fourteen." The tone of his voice changed, as if he were remembering a dream. "Yvette Lopez. I met her one summer in Mexico. She couldn't speak much English, so that was in my favor." He chuckled at his memory.

I sat up, pulling my legs onto the bench and wrapping my arms around them.

"I cheated on a math test once," I said. "I just wanted to see if I could do it and not get caught." I shuddered. I'd been so scared, thinking I would get in trouble and the teacher would give me an F. But nothing happened, except that I felt like crap about it for a couple of weeks.

"I tried to steal a CD from Target, but a clerk caught me."

"And?" I asked.

"They called my parents and threatened to call the cops, but the manager let me go with a warning. I was grounded for a week."

"What CD was it?"

He smiled and turned away.

"Come on. It's confession time." I jabbed him in the ribs.

"Shania Twain."

"No way!"

Defending himself, Tyler said, "I like all kinds of music."

I blurted out, "I used to hit Micah to make him cry, and then deny it to my parents and say that he had hit me. I was a terrible sister."

"Again, another benefit of being an only child." He smiled, becoming quiet. His hands played with the frays at the end of his jeans. "Not really. As an only child, you also have to keep secrets between parents. There's more of a buffer if there are other kids. Last year I walked in on my mom and this other guy. I'd left school early for some reason, and there she was, and there he was, doing it in the living room."

I was stunned.

"Believe me, that is one thing you never want to see." He smiled again, but I saw the pain behind it.

"Does your dad know?"

Tyler shook his head. "No. I never talked about it to my mom, either. That night she made my dad's favorite meal and we moved on."

"That's terrible. I'm so sorry."

"No family is perfect."

Accepting truth was like removing a Band-Aid: at first it was painful, then it left a red mark and some of that gray sticky gunk that you had to scrape off.

"I never told my parents where Micah kept his stash or when he was high or that I knew that he was using all along. I should have told them," I said. "It could have helped."

Tyler started to interrupt me, but I held up my hand.

"The longer it went on, the deeper Micah got, the more I wanted it all to go away. It got to where I couldn't sleep because I was so stressed." My voice flickered like one of the candles. "I started to wish that he would just disappear, so I wouldn't have to deal with him anymore. When he first left, I was relieved, but then . . ." The weight of the guilt that I had carried since Micah disappeared made it hard for me to continue.

"It's not your fault. This thing with Micah, all of it has been his choosing."

"I know, but—"

He cut me off. "Listen, Micah was like a brother to me, at least what I imagine a brother to be. We fought, yet I always knew he had my back. He's the one who left. You didn't push him away. I love him too, but he has to be the one to decide when he's had enough. Your guilt isn't going to bring him back any sooner."

"I . . ." I tried to speak, but I felt tears welling in my eyes. "It's just . . . his room is like this open tomb back there, and my parents . . . they can't handle it. They hardly talk anymore, to me, to each other. I'm still their daughter, but I might as well have left too. It's like I meant nothing to Micah. It's always silent, and sometimes I feel like I can't breathe." I was crying now. "I thought that if I could find Micah, I could fix everything. That we could go back to the way things used to be. I could find some sense of normal."

Tyler stood up and walked to the back of the room.

Great, I thought. *Now I've upset him. Maybe he can't handle a girl crying, and he'll leave too.*

He reappeared beside me. "Here." He handed me a couple of tissues. "There's a bathroom back there."

"Thank you." I wiped my eyes and blew my nose. I looked around the candlelit room. "Do you ever pray?"

The question seemed to catch him off guard. "Sometimes, I guess."

"I don't really know any prayers," I said.

Tyler picked up one of the books on the bench. "Here's a whole bunch." He flipped through, then closed it. "Probably not what you're looking for." He put the book back down. "When my dad was going through his program, working his steps, he prayed. He said he started talking to the Big Guy. Maybe you should just say what you need to say."

As if to help me get started, Tyler sat back on the bench and closed his eyes.

I closed my eyes and thought of the name I used when I was a kid. "So, Frank . . . I'm angry. No, I'm pissed off. I came all the way down here to San Diego. I lied to my parents. My car got stolen. Some crazy drug dealer could have killed us. But I thought that we'd find Micah, like you'd help me or something. Instead, this has all been one big waste of time." I stopped speaking and counted to six to calm myself before I began again. "Is all of this worth it? What's the point?"

I opened my eyes and looked at the large Jesus, at His tormented face, His contorted body. Why was He always hanging on a cross? Why didn't they ever take Him off the damn thing? What kind of people came to this place week after week to stare at Him like that? Were they sadists? Did it make them feel better to see His suffering? Kind of like when I got a little happy when I heard that someone else was having a worse day than I was?

I couldn't see the color of the statue's eyes from where I sat, but I pictured Micah's eyes, my eyes—a deep reddish brown. The blood from Jesus's hands flowed, joining the wound in His side and continuing down His legs. So much blood. Micah was killing himself and there was nothing I could do. I just wanted to know why.

Jesus hung there, staring at me in all His agony, and I suddenly understood something: Everyone suffered. Micah took drugs. I had chosen the wrong guy. Tyler kept secrets. A dealer got beaten to a pulp. But it was more than that. Sometimes we had to walk through the pain alone. I looked back at a picture on the wall, the one where a bystander helped Jesus carry the cross. Sometimes we had others to help us along the way.

I remembered the prayer from Micah's rehab group. "God

grant me the serenity to accept the things I cannot change, courage to change the things I can, and wisdom to know the difference."

"Amen," Tyler said.

"Amen."

I lay down on the bench. I didn't want to think or talk anymore. I just needed sleep. But another thought came to mind.

"What am I going to tell my parents about the car?"

"The truth is usually less complicated." Tyler got up and started blowing out the candles.

When he was finished, I think he came back to where I was lying. I was almost asleep.

"I never made my last confession," he said softly.

"Hmm? You can tell me in the morning," I mumbled.

"Technically, it is morning." He paused. "Keith was a bastard who never realized the gift he'd been given."

I didn't say anything, because it was true and I was ready to let that one go. I fell asleep.

Chapter Twenty-Six

My muscles were sore when I woke. I should have known that the pew bench, if not comfortable to sit on, would definitely not be the best substitute for a bed. The hazy morning light told me that it was still early. Red choir robes covered me. I smiled. Tyler must have got them. The last thing I remembered was talking with Tyler. Where was he?

I looked around and found him in the row behind me, stretched out on his back, looking more comfortable than I was. The brim of his cap was pulled down low over his face, covering everything except his chin.

I reached over and gave him a push. He grunted. I pushed him again.

"Okay. Okay. I'm up." In one motion, he sat up and rubbed

his eyes. He ran his fingers through his black hair. He noticed me watching him. "Don't you look lovely in the morning?"

"Save it," I said. "I'm going to the bathroom. We'd better leave before someone comes."

In the bathroom mirror, I grimaced at my bed head. Using my fingers as a comb, I tried to tame my hair, but that didn't really work. I pulled it into a ponytail and went to the bathroom. I splashed some water on my face and pinched my cheeks. Instant blush. At least I looked clean and healthy. Not bad for being out all night.

Tyler was at the door when I exited.

"My turn," he said.

I stepped aside for him to pass, and I felt a little awkward. It felt intimate spending the night together, but not spending the night together. Something had changed between us. It wasn't anything I could say for certain, just a sense of a new beginning.

"Excuse me," I said, flustered.

He smiled, and this time I didn't fight the disarming effect.

I turned back toward the main room of the church. Gone was the somber and medieval vibe. Sunlight streaked through the stained glass windows. I walked to the center of the room and held my hand up to touch one of the beams, almost expecting it to burn right through my palm. I like mornings because each day is like another chance.

I fixated on a large window near the front. I hadn't noticed it in the dark, but in the light of day it stood out from the other mosaics.

It was a picture of Jesus rising in the air. A halo of light encircled His head. People knelt in front of Him. He looked calm and peaceful. He wasn't suffering anymore. I glanced up at the hanging Jesus and smiled, knowing that He would eventually make it through.

"You ready?" Tyler asked from behind me.

I stood with the sunlight on my fingertips for a few moments more. "Yeah."

Holding a package of small, plain cake doughnuts under my arm, with my free hand, I opened the store's refrigerator door to get something to drink. I pulled out some kind of vitamin drink, but the ingredients revealed that it was just as sugary as soda. I put it back. It didn't really matter because of the doughnuts, but I had to draw the line somewhere. I had already blown my soda boycott at lunch with Tyler. I chose a nondescript bottle of water instead.

Tyler was busy using one of the coffee tumblers on the other side of the store. I had learned that he took his coffee black. He seemed more of a man for it. He turned and caught my eye from across the way and mouthed did I want one. I shook my head.

The man sitting at the register watched the news on a tiny TV that hung in the corner. Apparently the traffic was already mounting up, and the day would be another warm one. Some chef would be on soon to explain how to cook the best barbeque chicken. Outside, a couple of cars were at the pumps getting gas, but we were the only people in the store.

Tyler approached me with his large coffee.

"I figured you for more of a powdered girl." He pointed to the doughnuts.

"Nope. Plain or glazed."

"Note taken."

I lowered my head, but smiled because it felt good that Tyler was taking notes on things that I liked.

"Of course, there's always Cheetos and CornNuts." He gestured to the next aisle of snacks.

I didn't know anyone who bought CornNuts, but there must have been people out there who were CornNut people. Why else would they stock the shelves with it?

"If you get the CornNuts, I will definitely not be riding back with you. CornNut breath is the worst."

"I'm starving. I need something more than doughnuts. Throw in two HotPockets."

I put two ham and cheese HotPockets into the microwave. The plan was to make our way back to the bus stop and take the next bus to a train station. From there, I knew that Tyler could probably get ahold of a friend at a pay phone. And I could get in touch with Michelle or someone else. Between the two of us, we had enough connections to find someone who could come and get us without having to call my parents. But neither of us said anything. I followed Tyler's lead. So far he hadn't let me down.

We placed our loot on the counter by the register. The door

opened. In the large mirror above the cashier, I saw two figures enter. As they moved, their bodies stretched in the reflection, becoming distorted and twisted like at a carnival fun house. I could tell they were men by their frames. For a second, I held my breath, as hope again reared its head.

I turned around slowly to get a better look at them. They both wore black hoodies. The one who wasn't wearing his hood up had brown hair and was about the same size as Micah. He looked right at me, and I couldn't stop the disappointment. He stared past me, and I quickly turned away. I released my breath slowly.

"You all right?" Tyler asked.

"Yeah, just tired."

I wondered if it would always be this way. If every time I heard a door open, I'd turn and look with both hope and fear. If I'd have that sinking feeling in my chest when it wasn't Micah. I wondered if there'd ever be a time when the sound of an opening door would be nothing more than that. Is that what it meant to move on, to let go?

Tyler gave the cashier his credit card. Thank goodness for that. He smiled and was about to say something, but I said it first.

"I know, only-child benefits."

I grabbed the bag of our "breakfast." We walked out into the morning sun. I stopped. I closed my eyes and lifted my face upward. My whole body flooded with warmth.

"Can you feel that?" I asked Tyler.

"What?" He stood in the shade of the store's sign.

"Here." I pulled him close so he could stand in the same spot as me. He was still and didn't say anything. I felt additional warmth with him so close.

Over at the pumps, a driver stood next to her blue SUV and talked on her cell phone. Another car stood alone at the pump. I could only see the rear because the rest of it was hidden behind the pump. It was small, nondescript, probably a Honda or Toyota. A spark of sunlight reflected off the black bumper.

A strange feeling came over me, making me want to get a better look. I crept closer. I was right. It was a Honda Civic, and there was a dent in the rear bumper. It was there when I bought the car. I knew that I'd find another dent on the left side. That one happened in a Vons parking lot. The culprit hadn't even left a note. I looked all around to see if anyone was watching, and then I remembered the guys in the store and got scared. A short brick wall separated the water and air tire service from the pumps. I ran and ducked behind it.

"Are you crazy?" Tyler asked me as he jogged after me and squatted down, almost spilling his coffee.

"That's my car!" My eyes were wide with shock.

"What?" Tyler peered at the car. "Are you sure?"

"Of course I'm sure."

Tyler looked again. "Looks like your car."

"I *know* it's my car." I said the words with a bit more of a bite than I had intended.

"Okay. It's your car." He looked toward the store. "Those guys in there must be with it."

"What are we gonna do?" I asked.

"Let me think for a second."

"We've got to call the cops or something."

He shook his head. "No time."

"There's a pay phone," I said, pointing to the black box standing close to the store's entrance.

"By the time we get ahold of the police, your car will be long gone."

I looked toward the convenience store. I could see only one of the men. He stood in front of the glass refrigerator doors. Suddenly I remembered something. "Or, we could use this." I fished in my backpack and removed my keys.

Tyler looked at me with surprise. "The key?"

I nodded.

He smiled wide.

"What if they have a gun or a knife or something?" I said.

"Maybe. Look, this could be our only chance. I'll creep over and start the car. You head over to the intersection, and I'll pick you up at the light and we'll get the hell out of here."

"What if you get caught?"

"I won't." He sounded too confident.

"I think I should do it," I said.

"No way! Too dangerous."

I wanted to roll my eyes at Tyler, but he was only trying to protect me. "Sometimes you have to fiddle with the ignition to start it. I know how to do it. You've never driven it."

He squinted at me, probably trying to decide if he should listen.

"If you can't start it right away, bail."

"Agreed. Can you still see them?"

Tyler looked back at the store. "Yeah, they're at the register. Give me that." He took my backpack and the bag of food. "If you're gonna do it, go now. I'll meet you at the corner." He stood up and moved quickly toward the street.

I sneaked slowly along the asphalt toward my car, keeping low to the ground. I could feel my heart pounding in my ears. I refused to look back at the store. It was better if I didn't see what could be coming.

Reaching the driver's side, I touched the familiar handle and pulled. The door was impossible to open from my crouching position. I had to stand up. I froze, literally paralyzed with fear. I couldn't move. This was the moment they might see me. My voice inside my head yelled to move, but I remained still.

I tried to focus. *One. Two. Three.* I counted. *Please God.*

Through the window I could see the car had been cleaned really well on the inside. All of my junk had been taken out of the backseat. *Four. Five.* The only clutter now was a pack of cigarettes on the front passenger seat. *Six. Please God. Seven.* I felt my body begin to relax. I stood up. My hand pulled on the lever and opened the door. I got inside.

Something was wrong. The seat. It was pushed back farther than I normally had it. I felt violated, but I didn't have time to adjust the seat. I put the key in the ignition, jiggled it right, then left, then right again. The car started.

The store door opened, and I saw the men walking in my direction. I freaked out. I stepped on the gas pedal and floored it. The tires squealed and something ripped and popped behind me. I had forgotten to unhook the gas pump.

The other woman at the pump screamed. The men started running toward me. I swerved out of their way, and the car bottomed out as it hit the street.

"Sorry!" I shouted to the car.

Tyler waved his free hand from the corner. I pulled up and slammed on my brakes. As soon as Tyler's body was in the car, I accelerated again. He pulled the door shut. I didn't know how close the guys were behind me, but I didn't want to take any chances.

The light had just turned red, but I braced myself and sped through it. Out of the corner of my eye, I saw a sign that said to turn right for the freeway ramp, and I took it like a speeding demon.

"Jesus, Rachel, you can slow down!" yelled Tyler.

A car honked as I almost sideswiped it. Entering and exiting the freeway were still weak spots in my driving.

"Okay, okay. I'm calming down. I'm calming down." But my hands gripped the steering wheel so tightly my knuckles were drained of color.

"You're going to kill us long before those guys get a chance," Tyler said, though he didn't sound upset. He burst out laughing. "You're crazy. You drove up so fast, I thought you were going to jump the curb and hit me. I had to ditch the coffee. You should have seen your face." He made some wild maniac face as he tried to imitate me.

"Oh yeah? Well, you didn't look too calm yourself."

Tyler made the face again, and I started to laugh. It was light at first, a kind of laugh to ease the nervous tension. It began to build when I thought about how insane it was that I'd stolen back my car. I laughed thinking about what those guys must have thought at the station. They were probably so pissed.

I laughed deeper and my whole body began to shake. I leaned over the steering wheel and my gut started to hurt. I couldn't stop. Tears began to form in the corners of my eyes.

"Stop it!" I said, as if it were Tyler's fault. He continued to laugh with me. It felt so good to laugh.

When we were kids, Micah and I would play a game where we'd do silly things to try and make the other person laugh. I always lost because Micah had no problem going to the extreme. He would take a straw and make the milk come out of his nose. Or he would make all of these weird and disgusting sounds with his body. Sometimes he'd get up and do the booty dance and shake his tush in the air and make some silly face until we were both on the floor laughing.

I wiped the tears with my hand and tried to focus on the road ahead of me. Tyler's laugh subsided. A silence, a small grace, rested between us.

"You laugh just like your brother," Tyler said.

"I know," I said, and smiled.

Chapter Twenty-Seven

Though traffic wound ahead of us, we made it to the parking lot where we had started our journey in a little over an hour. Tyler's truck was waiting. I pulled up next to it and turned off the engine.

"Thank you for coming with me," I said.

"You're welcome." He remained in his seat, looking out the front windshield.

"Sorry about all the drama. It's not what I anticipated."

He laughed. "Made things interesting, that's for sure." He made no move to go. "Rachel, I have to tell you something."

He said the words the way someone does when they're about to tell you that they just ran over your dog.

"What?" I tried to sound casual.

"It's something I didn't say at the church." He continued to stare ahead. "The truth is, I am kind of glad that Micah went missing."

I looked at him in surprise.

He turned to me. "If Micah hadn't left, then you wouldn't have called me and we wouldn't be here today." He kind of rushed the words together. "I wanted a chance to be alone with you."

I didn't expect him to say that. "You barely know me."

"Are you serious? I've known you for forever, since fifth grade."

"Yeah, but—"

"I know you." He said the words softly.

"Why didn't you ever say anything?"

"You're Micah's little sister. You know how much shit I'd take for it?" He chuckled when he said it.

"Probably a lot."

Suddenly the car felt too warm in the heat of the sun, so I opened my door and got out. I leaned back against the hood and closed my eyes. Tyler's door opened and shut. Then he stood next to me.

"What're you thinking?" he asked.

Thinking is overrated, I thought. I didn't want to admit it, but I was afraid of where things with Tyler could lead. I was afraid of getting hurt again.

"I should call my mom," I said. "She'll be wondering what my plans are for the day."

"Oh." His voice sounded dejected. "Yeah, you should probably call her."

I felt bad. I didn't mean to act like I was brushing off what he'd told me. Such a raw admission of truth deserved at least the same response in kind.

"It's just . . . weird. Micah . . ."

"Micah," he said.

We stayed quiet for a few moments, leaning against my car.

"Well, at least you got your miracle today."

"What's that?" I asked.

"You got your car back."

He was right. I hadn't thought of it that way.

"Hey, you never told me your miracle." I looked into his eyes playfully, hoping he'd see I was interested.

Instead of answering, he put on his sunglasses and said, "Some other time. I'll see ya." He walked over to his truck.

As he opened the driver's side door, I decided to take a step toward a more authentic self. "Tyler." He turned around. "I could have asked anyone to come with me. I asked you."

He smiled. "Call you later?"

I nodded, and he ducked his head inside his truck.

He pulled out of the parking lot, and I picked up my cell phone. Amazingly, everything in the glove compartment had been left untouched. I saw that I had about ten texts from Michelle. She could wait a little longer. I dialed a number.

"Mom?" I said when she answered.

"Hi, Rachel." Her voice sounded tired. "Did you have a good time?"

"Yeah, I just wanted you to know that I'm on my way home."

I hung up the phone and started the car.

Later that night, after spending at least an hour on the phone, filling Michelle in on the details of Operation San Diego, as I was now calling it, I decided to e-mail Micah. I doubted he'd get it, but I couldn't help it. I was a sucker for closure.

Dear Micah,

Tyler and I went looking for you yesterday down by that beach you love. I found bits and pieces of you in the people we met, and I think this is how it will be for a while. The bits and pieces will find me until the whole of you is ready to find its way home.

Thank you for sticking up for me with Keith. Finn told me. For what it's worth, I think she really loves you.

I want you to know that I'm not going to look for you. I'm not going to write to you again. This will be my last e-mail. I am letting you go.

Love,

Rachel

I pressed send and released the e-mail into cyberspace like a prayer. On the table next to my bed was my small notebook with

Micah's picture. I opened it to yesterday's date and crossed off pretty much everything on my list. I paused for a moment at *Find Micah*. But I crossed that off as well, and wrote tomorrow's date on a new page.

I took Micah's picture and placed it inside a small frame that had held a goofy picture of some friends and me. It fit perfectly.

My phone beeped. It was a message from Tyler.

Night.

I smiled. If anything about the trip had surprised me, it was Tyler.

Night, I texted back.

I got under the covers. Pale moonlight streamed in through my unveiled window and shone through a couple of dirty smudges, like stained glass. Barely visible but still there was *MS*. Micah's initials. Mine were there too, a little beneath his, right where they should have been.

Acknowledgments

No work of art lives and breathes without being shaped by many hands. For that I am profoundly grateful.

To my superagent, Kerry Sparks, who saw the potential and said yes. This book would be stashed away on a lonely flash drive if not for you.

To the team at Simon Pulse, who welcomed me and believed. Emilia Rhodes, whose initial enthusiastic notes started me on the journey. My wonderful editor, Annette Pollert, whose insight and care with this story has made it better than I ever could have on my own.

To friends and family who supported me. Michelle Dokolas, for being someone with whom I share the news first. Your encouragement and critiques were like water. Ted and Judy Lawler, my parents, who taught me to follow big, impossible, God-inspired dreams and make them possible.

And finally, to my husband, David. You are the dream maker. This is as much yours as it is mine. Thank you, my love.

Aiden, Matisse, and Judah—this is proof. Dreams can come true.